Summer Rose

The Sutton Book Club

Katie Winters

Chapter One

The last day of Rebecca's life was a lot like the rest of them—busy. As head chef of Maine's estimable Bar Harbor Brasserie, she set her Saturday alarm for five thirty and woke with just enough time to brew herself a piping-hot cup of coffee, get dressed in the dark, kiss Fred's cheek as he sleepily whispered he loved her, and rush off for the fish market. As usual, there was no time to waste. Everything had to happen on time or not at all.

If she'd known it was the last day, would she have slowed down? Spent another few minutes in bed? Gathered her family together at the breakfast table for cinnamon rolls and a final laugh? There was no way to ever know this. That was the nature of time. You could never get it back.

The fish market on the edge of town opened at six. Although it was January and months from Bar Harbor's tourist season, chefs and restaurateurs scavenged the market early for the best cuts of seafood and bright red lobsters. That morning, Rebecca had to fight tooth and nail to get the very finest because the governor of Maine planned to dine at her restaurant that night. He'd chosen her restaurant and not any of the other popular establishments across Bar Harbor. This was a privilege and an honor, yes, but that didn't mean it didn't terrify Rebecca to her core.

Fred Vance, Rebecca's favorite person and the love of her life, was also her restaurant manager, which was usually a good thing. Usually. Regarding the governor, Fred had suggested this dinner and its photo opportunities could make the difference between being a "great" restaurant and being one of the "best."

As the fish and lobster procured, safely layered with ice in a cooler in the back of her SUV, Rebecca called Fred. As soon as she heard his groggy hello, she said, "I don't know if I'm up for this."

She could feel Fred's smile through the phone. "Are you kidding me? You're Rebecca Vance. I've never seen you fail."

"What if I do, Freddy? I mean, this is a huge deal. The governor! Why did he choose our restaurant?"

"Because you're a renowned chef in the Maine culinary scene? Because he likes good food?" Fred paused and chuckled to himself. "Because he wants to make you miserable."

"I knew it," Rebecca muttered.

"Listen. If you mess something up, we'll take the kids, move to the Keys, and go into hiding," Fred said. "Didn't you say, as long as you're cooking, you could be happy anywhere? You can open a taco stand."

Rebecca groaned but soon heard herself laugh, grateful for the easy way Fred looked at the world. Her anxiety had always needed his calm.

"So. What's going on there?" Rebecca asked. "Is Shelby up yet?"

"I hear her puttering around up there," Fred said.

"Good. Tell her I'll be back to pick her up by seven thirty. Tell her not to forget her ID!"

"It's already here on the table where you put it last night."

"Right."

"Why don't you take a few deep breaths for me?" Fred suggested.

"I would never do that for you," Rebecca joked. She hovered at a red light, closed her eyes, and focused on inhaling, then slowly exhaling.

Fred explained he was heading to the restaurant, where he had to do payroll. Rebecca told him she loved him, then asked him twice if he was sure he could attend Chad's basketball game that night and come back to the restaurant afterward to thank the governor for his time. Fred answered, *"yes,"* and then, *"don't ask me again."* He told her he loved her three times because he knew her mind raced too quickly for her to hear it the first time. The third time was just a bonus.

Shelby was the middle Vance child and a junior in high school. Today, of all days, she'd signed up to take the SATs for the second time. During her first attempt back in autumn, she'd had a mild panic attack midway through the math section and hid in the bathroom for five minutes as the supervisor had knocked on the door, demanding she come back. Needless to say, the scores hadn't matched what all the Vances knew Shelby was capable of.

Rebecca opened the door between the garage and the kitchen and found her daughter at the counter with a piece of toast and a knife covered in peanut butter. "Do you have your ID?"

Shelby rolled her eyes. "Yes, Mom. I have my ID. Just because Lily forgot hers four years ago doesn't mean I'll do the same."

"You say it like it wasn't the biggest disaster of 2018." Rebecca checked the coffee pot, which Fred had graciously restocked, and poured herself another helping.

Chad made his way down the staircase with all his taut muscles and electric energy. Wearing a pair of basketball shorts and an all-American smile, he kissed Rebecca on the cheek, then hollered, "I'm going out for breakfast with the team!"

"Put on real pants!" Rebecca called after him. She rubbed her temples as Shelby laughed. After three sips of her coffee, she pointed her thumb toward the garage. "We're leaving in five. I'm going to check on your sister. Okay?"

Before Shelby could answer, Rebecca was on the staircase. On mornings like these, she felt like a bird, fluttering through events and responsibilities in her life and praying not to flatten herself against a window. Outside her eldest daughter's bedroom, she listened intently and finally found the sound of her daughter's deep breathing. Just a week ago, Lily had called from Columbia University with a terrible diagnosis. It was mono and had already wiped out half her dormitory floor. "Mom? Can you pick me up?" she'd croaked. *When it rained, it poured.*

"Lily's still sleeping, thank goodness," Rebecca reported to Shelby in the front seat of the SUV. Shelby's nails clacked over her phone screen, and Rebecca again considered the fact that she shouldn't have gotten phones for her children at such a young age. *Were they too devoted to technology? Had she deprived them of a wonderful youth? Then again, was there anything you could ever do to stop progress in the world?*

Shelby hustled from the SUV to the front door of the high school. She paused to wave back at her mother and then disappeared into the shadows. Rebecca sent a necessary "just dropped Shelby off" text to Fred, who sent back a thumbs-up. Often, they joked they were the only two teammates in a tremendously complicated video game. It was them versus the world.

Rebecca parked the SUV in the back parking lot of Bar Harbor Brasserie, which she and Fred had opened ten years ago when their children had been eleven, seven, and six. Friends had asked if they were insane. Dave, her sous chef, bustled from the back and waved a sturdy hand, ready to help her with the fish coolers. Rebecca had already sent him twelve frantic text messages, hoping to illustrate just how important today was for the future of Bar Harbor Brasserie. It wasn't hard to get Dave excited about something. If Fred and Rebecca were the heart and soul of the restaurant, Dave was the respiratory system that kept them breathing.

"Today's the big day!" Dave swung open the back of the SUV and grabbed the cooler with ease.

"You make it sound like a celebration." Rebecca laughed as she closed the SUV, then hustled out in front of him to open the back of the restaurant.

"Isn't it? I mean, the governor picked our restaurant out of all the Bar Harbor restaurants to dine at," Dave continued. He showed no strain from the weight of the enormous cooler.

"You know how I feel about too much optimism in my kitchen. It makes the fish stink," Rebecca teased.

As Dave set aside the fish for the lunch rush and the evening courses, Rebecca breezed past the office to wave to Fred through the window. Fred waved back, a pen between his lips. She then scrubbed her hands, donned a hairnet and an apron, and began to prep potatoes as if her life depended on it. Ordinarily, she asked the kitchen staff to do this, but with her anxiety through the roof and about ten other things to prep for the night ahead, she'd decided to give herself the gift of peeling, washing, and slicing. It was meditative, reminiscent of her early days at culinary school. Back then, she hadn't been married or had children. All she'd had were her dreams and a million potatoes before her.

In the middle of the lunch rush, Rebecca put Dave in charge and rushed back to Mount Desert High School to pick up Shelby from her second attempt at the SAT. Once she limped to the SUV, Shelby's lower lip bounced around tragically as she explained what had gone wrong this time. Rebecca held her daughter against her chest for as long as her schedule allowed it, then a few seconds longer, before she announced that Shelby could retake the SATs as many times as she wanted to. "You'll do it until it feels right." She then traced the familiar path back to their family home, where Shelby planned to hide in bed and pretend the morning hadn't happened. "I wish I could join you, honey," Rebecca joked.

Lily had managed to throw herself downstairs and onto the living room couch, where she was plastered beneath a mountain of blankets. Shelby waved dully and disappeared upstairs as Lily blew her Rudolph nose.

"Oh, my poor baby." Rebecca adjusted the blankets over Lily's frail body. "Do you feel any better?"

"Not really," Lily explained. "But the walls of my

bedroom were closing in. I had to watch TV in a different place."

Lily turned off her streaming platform, and the weather station took back over the television. The weatherman waved his authoritative hand over a smattering of snow clouds and smiled. Rebecca hadn't known the forecast. *Ten inches of snow before midnight? Would the governor still make it?* Then again, this was Maine, so snow was a given. The governor himself called Maine residents "hardy stock."

Lily groaned and stretched her arms over her head. "How's it going at the restaurant?"

Rebecca flopped onto the edge of the couch. "Let's just say I don't have time to sit here with you. But I'm too exhausted to stand right now."

"You have to take care of yourself, Mom," Lily scolded her.

"Says the girl who got mono at a wild college party."

"Maybe I got it there, or maybe I didn't. And I never should have told you about that." Lily feigned anger but was too exhausted to rise to it.

"Relax, honey. I'm glad you have friends down there," Rebecca said. "But more than that, I'm glad you're here with me for a little while."

The weather channel went to a commercial. In the first, a little boy ate cereal with his grandfather, who imparted early morning wisdom. In the second, a water bowl for cats refilled itself when it was empty, at least until the larger basin ran dry. And in the third, a talk show host advertised her next guest—an accomplished and respected family and children's psychologist named Victor Sutton.

"You know him. You love him. And more than that,

you need his advice," the talk show host said of Victor Sutton. "Many of you tuned in over a year ago when I last spoke with Victor as he helped me through the dark days of my divorce and custody hearing. It was incredibly difficult for me to open myself up to my viewers, but I know it brought many of you closer to living better and more fulfilling lives. I think I speak for both Victor and me when I say that's why we do what we do."

Rebecca snorted. Rage bubbled through her stomach and filled her chest. *Victor Sutton? The brilliant family and children's psychologist? Victor Sutton? The helper and healer? Had the world gone completely crazy?*

"Sorry." Lily changed the station quickly and flashed her mother a worried glance.

"You have nothing to be sorry about," Rebecca affirmed. "Watch whatever you want and sit tight. I'm going to make you a big bowl of soup. How does that sound?"

"The other kids with mono don't have personal chefs at home," Lily pointed out. "Should I pity them? Or rub this into their faces even more?"

Rebecca laughed and hurried to the kitchen, grateful for something else to do with her anxious mind. As she sliced garlic and onions, she tried her best to blink out the image of Victor Sutton, whom she hadn't seen since she was a teenager. No, she hadn't invited him to Maine for her wedding, nor after any of the births of her children. But by then, she'd gotten so close with Fred's family that it hadn't mattered. She was no longer a Sutton. It was over.

Before Rebecca left for the afternoon, Chad breezed through the front door. She wished him a final good luck on his game later, and he high-fived her with a dirty hand.

She grimaced. "I'm cooking the governor's meal with these hands later!"

Chad laughed. "Haven't you heard of soap, Mom?"

Rebecca did her best to focus. The governor planned to dine at Bar Harbor Brasserie at seven thirty sharp, which was a half hour after Chad's basketball game began. All of the other tables in the restaurant were booked for the night, which would allow Bar Harbor Brasserie to show off the impressive beauty of their other dishes. Rebecca prayed that nobody in the restaurant that evening would bother the governor. Her worst nightmare was that someone would demand answers about this recent tax bill just as the servers brought him the first course. Regardless of what you thought of his politics, the governor was a good man—and he loved Bar Harbor.

And who didn't love Bar Harbor? It had been Rebecca's chosen home since her early twenties. Sometimes at night, she dreamed of the beaches she'd once known on Nantucket, of the calm waters along the Nantucket Sound and the gentle beauty of Nantucket's fields of daffodils. But more often, she thanked her lucky stars for Maine's Acadia Mountains, its rocky coastlines, and its quiet yet compassionate people. Fred was from Maine, and he was the single greatest person she'd ever known. After years of torment, depression, and loneliness, meeting him had been like coming home.

The kitchen bustled with staff. Servers rushed around, adjusting their aprons and instructing the younger members to provide the best fine dining service. However, this benefited Rebecca's restaurant's reputation because Rebecca had always found it astounding how demeaning some of the more seasoned servers could get. She flashed one of her favorite staff members a warning glance, and as a result, the server backpedaled on her strictness, ultimately telling the younger girl to "just have fun out there."

Rebecca had decided to flaunt her skills for the governor's multicourse dinner. She would begin with an appetizer of smoked salmon mousse, followed by pasta with lobster sauce, seafood risotto, pan-fried sea bass with lemon garlic herb sauce, and a crème brûlée. When she'd asked Fred's opinion of the menu, he'd fallen to his knees and said, "Let's close the restaurant on Sunday and enjoy that meal ourselves. When was the last time we sat together and enjoyed dinner, just us?" To this, Rebecca had joked, "I knew you would lose your mind over the seafood risotto."

Around six, amid Rebecca's prepping flurry, Fred appeared to kiss her good luck.

"Are you going to pick up Chad?" Rebecca had her fingers coated in lobster sauce.

"He has a ride to the basketball court," Fred explained.

"Okay. Great. Send me updates from the game, okay?"

Fred saluted her and kissed her again.

"The governor should be gone by ten or so. Afterward, we can celebrate."

"How do you want to celebrate?" Fred asked.

"With the biggest glass of Cabernet Bar Harbor has ever seen."

"Count me in. I love you, by the way. Whatever happens tonight, remember, you're the best chef Bar Harbor has ever seen."

"And we can always run away and open that taco stand. I know."

With Fred gone, the kitchen chugged along like a powerful machine. Diners had begun to arrive, and servers sent their orders back to the kitchen. The air was frantic and bubbling. Dave barked at a few kitchen members to chop faster. Rebecca stirred the lobster sauce and took deep breaths. As a way to ground herself in facts, she tried to remember everything she could about the governor. He'd gone to Columbia, just like her daughter. His wife's name was Brenda. They had a black Labrador named Snoopy. Their children were grown up, perhaps ten years older than hers. *Oh, but what did this matter? All that mattered was he liked the food.* No—he couldn't just like the food. He had to adore it. He had to tell everyone he'd ever met about it. Only then could she and Fred claim victory.

"Boss. You have to see the snow." Dave bustled in from a smoke break and brushed the white flakes from his shoulders.

Rebecca's stomach lurched. *Would the governor still make it?* She hurried to the back doorway to take in the glorious view of thick, wet snowflakes that piled on the roofs of cars and twinkled beneath the streetlights. A winter wonderland in the truest sense. Maybe, if he did make it, the sensational view out the front window would make the governor remember this night at Bar Harbor Brasserie that much more.

Unafraid of snowfall, the governor of Maine arrived five minutes early and announced to the server that he and his wife, Brenda, were famished. In the kitchen, Rebecca set to work, keeping to her rule of not introducing herself until after an important guest had finished his or her meal. She needed to see the look in their eyes afterward as proof she'd succeeded.

First came the smoked salmon mousse, served with freshly baked bread and house-made crackers. This paired exquisitely with the wine, which the server had suggested—a one-hundred-and-twelve-dollar bottle from southern Germany. On a rare vacation, Fred and Rebecca had traveled to a number of German wineries to complete their white wine selection. At the time, they'd left the restaurant in Dave's capable hands but spent nearly every day worrying, as though the restaurant was their last remaining infant. In a way, it was.

Three courses went out, then the fourth. The governor's server reported the governor was clearly enjoying himself and had even asked a few questions about the locally sourced products and the flavor pairings. "He's a man who knows what he likes," the server explained. "And I think it's safe to say he likes your stuff."

"Don't jinx us. The night isn't over till it's over," Rebecca said.

Oh, but she felt as though she floated above the kitchen. She felt fully aware and capable in everything she did, as though every moment of her career had led to this second. She dared to imagine herself a year or two from then, perhaps at a bigger restaurant or even a brand-new location in a bigger city. Couldn't she compete with the New York City ranks? Couldn't she see herself among the best of the very best?

Maybe that was going too far. But if there was any time rife for daydreaming, it was now. She scorched the bottom of the crème brûlée dish and watched as the top hardened to a beautiful sliver of sugar. Then she took the fire to it next. Servers breezed in and out of the kitchen doors, their arms ladened with Rebecca's creations. Soon, the governor's dinner would be finished. Soon, she would pour the biggest glass of wine known to man and collapse in Fred's arms.

Speaking of Fred, where was he? Rebecca had lost all concept of time. As the server took the crème brûlée out to the governor's table, she tried to get to her cell phone, which she'd left in the office. But as she weaved her way there, Dave and the other kitchen staffers stepped in with high fives and congratulations.

"That was the night of your life," Dave said. He wore an almost cartoonishly big smile. "You deserve every accolade. Seriously."

"You should have seen the governor's face when he cracked the crème brûlée!" The server arrived back from the dining room and punched Rebecca lightly on the upper arm. "He looked like a little kid."

Rebecca closed her eyes and exhaled all the air from her lungs. "I can't believe it's really over." She then clapped her hands. "Now, has anyone seen Fred? We have a date."

The staff members said they hadn't seen him. One suggested the basketball game had run long; another said maybe Fred had chatted with another high school parent for too long and lost track of time. God knew how Fred liked to chat. At first, Rebecca shrugged it off. But when she got into her office and saw a text from Fred from forty-five minutes ago, explaining he was on his way from the basketball game, Rebecca was no longer sure how to breathe. The drive from Mount Desert High School to Bar Harbor Brasserie took no longer than twelve minutes. In this snow, twenty tops.

"Hey, Chef? The governor wants to thank you personally for the meal." The server knocked against the doorway and smiled.

Rebecca tried to match the server's grin. She staggered through the kitchen and paused in front of the ever-whipping kitchen door. There, she told herself a story of optimism and hope. Nothing bad could happen to Rebecca Vance, right? She'd gotten her dark years out of the way as Rebecca Sutton.

But when she stepped into the dining room to claim her victory, everything in the world shifted so far off its axis that life as Rebecca knew it from that point on was no longer recognizable.

The governor sat with his wife at their best table, sipping the last of his wine and smiling lovingly. It was clear, at least for tonight, that whatever trouble politics had brought to their marriage wouldn't come to the forefront. They truly loved each other, even now. Rebecca respected that.

Across the dining room, Bar Harbor regulars and tourists championed Rebecca's seafood courses. They drank and laughed and swapped stories, their faces illuminated by the candlelight. The entire dining room evoked the very magic Rebecca had always wanted to create in a space of her own. She and Fred had been successful in this and so many other ways.

But in the foyer, speaking to the lead hostess, stood two police officers. They were damp with snow, and their faces were blotchy, their lips downturned. It took Rebecca a full minute to realize she knew them. Chance and Billy were a couple of local guys who'd gone to high school with Fred. They'd gone to his bachelor party. They'd gotten them a crappy blender for their wedding present, which had broken three weeks later.

And now, Chance and Billy lifted their eyes to hers with such pity and sorrow that she nearly toppled over.

Rebecca shook her head while the bottom dropped out beneath her. Someone, maybe Dave, placed his hand on her shoulder to hold her in place. Chance and Billy approached, and the lead hostess scrambled up behind them, sobbing tears that didn't belong to her.

"Honey." Rebecca heard her own voice as she reached out to take the lead hostess by the shoulder. "You should really go home tonight, okay? Before the roads get too bad."

The hostess quivered and stared at Rebecca as though Rebecca was the craziest woman on earth. Rebecca would soon learn that once the world labeled you as pitiable, it no longer respected you. Once the world labeled you as a widow, it did everything it could to pretend it didn't look down on you, even as it did. You were no longer a part of the story; yours remained in the past.

Chapter Two

Five Months Later

L ily's apartment building a few blocks from
Columbia University was a minefield of memories. Rebecca hadn't expected that. It was unfair,
really, as she and Fred had spent little more than a few
hours here in total. What had they done there, really?
They'd helped Lily unpack, set up her Wi-Fi, and tried to
impart the last of their wisdom before sending her back
into the world untethered. Nothing too emotional.
Nothing too enormous. But as Rebecca entered the apartment building to pick Lily up on the last day of the
semester, memories tore through her—of Fred carrying
boxes, Fred making jokes, Fred eating M&Ms from a
vending machine as Lily and Rebecca argued about how
short her skirt was.

"This is Columbia! Not a bar!"

"Mom, don't shame me!"

Rebecca had to disappear into the bathroom to clean

herself up before she faced her daughter. Lily had to think Rebecca was doing better because Rebecca had to be the brave face of their family.

Lily's apartment door was open. Inside, Lily and her roommate chatted in low and bored tones about a guy who'd been "so annoying" at a party. Rebecca tried to remember how long it had taken her to stop acting cool in front of her friends and start acting like herself.

"Hi! Is anyone home?" Rebecca knocked, and the two of them bounced from the couch and greeted her with perfumed hugs. It was the same perfume, as though they'd just sprayed it a few minutes before.

Lily had already packed her suitcases. She looked tanned and healthy and hugged her roommate three times before Rebecca could convince her to go. Lily's eyes welled with tears as they loaded the suitcases in the back of the SUV and fought through traffic. A beautiful spring sun shimmered upon them, a little hotter than normal at eighty-two degrees. It was hard to believe it was over.

"How did finals go?" Rebecca asked, imagining herself as a normal mother who picked up her normal daughter after a very normal semester.

"Oh, fine. History was the toughest because it was all essays. English was fine. We had two weeks to finish a fifteen-page paper on Jane Austen."

"You must have loved that," Rebecca said.

Lily glanced at her mother. In the past five months, she'd matured slightly. There was a sorrow in her eyes that had almost completely robbed Rebecca of her very first little girl. Grief did that to you. It took everything you had.

"But how are you doing?" Lily demanded.

Rebecca wasn't sure how to answer. So many people asked her that question every week that she'd developed canned responses. But could she lie to her daughter? Then again, wasn't lying a part of her campaign to show a brave face?

Instead of answering, she said, "In two weeks, Mindy Collins wants me to open the restaurant for one night only."

Lily frowned. "Why?"

"As a fundraiser for our family." Rebecca hated how her voice wavered.

"Mom? Do we need money?"

"It's not so bad," Rebecca tried to explain. "But obviously, we don't have the income we used to have."

"Mom, you can't do this," Lily said.

Rebecca stiffened. At the next stoplight, she turned to look at her daughter. "What do you mean?"

"I mean, you haven't stepped foot in that restaurant in months. Won't it be too painful to go in there without Dad?"

Rebecca had, of course, considered this. Each time she lifted the phone to tell Mindy the deal was off, Fred's voice entered her head, teasing her for how silly she was. *"What are you afraid of? That my ghost is there, waiting for you? Come on, Rebecca. You're a big girl. What's more, you were put on this earth to cook, weren't you? Get out there and show them what you're made of!"*

Shelby and Chad were both at home to welcome Lily. Shelby had baked a cake, which Chad had attempted to decorate with the logo for Columbia University.

"I guess we know who's not going into art," Shelby joked.

"There are wonderful bakers who could never be

pastry chefs," Rebecca reminded them. "Aesthetics aren't everyone's goal. And, if I'm not mistaken, this icing tastes delicious." She swiped the edge of her finger against the side of the cake as her children yelped in protest. When she tasted it, she closed her eyes and whispered, "Yep. It's great. Wonderful work, my darlings."

"Thanks, Chef!" Shelby and Chad cried in unison, which made Lily laugh. Although this wasn't the same uproarious energy of their original family, it echoed with it. It made everyone miss Fred that much more. Even the chair across the table seemed to wait expectantly for him.

For dinner, Rebecca ordered a stack of pizzas. Her children were in front of the television, watching a show from Rebecca's own youth and arguing over who the best characters were.

"You're such a Phoebe, Lily," Shelby said.

"That's a compliment," Lily returned. "Phoebe is weird and wonderful."

"Don't tell me I'm Ross," Chad groused.

"You're not. You're Joey," Shelby announced.

"Oh no." Chad considered this, perhaps finding it even worse.

Rebecca smiled to herself from the kitchen. Fred had always adored his children. For a few years, he'd even made the case they should have more. "Three is plenty if we want to open our own restaurant," Rebecca had insisted. Now, she couldn't help but imagine who that fourth or fifth child in their family would have been. More people would have meant more of Fred left behind. She'd taken to smelling his shirts at night, praying the scent would never fade.

The crash itself had been almost too simple. A life-long driver on snowy Maine roads, Fred had taken a turn too quickly and crashed into a tree. Life had a way of showing you just how little you understood about anything and that freak accidents could crop up whenever they pleased. Afterward, Rebecca had hardly driven all winter long and had sequestered herself at home, barely managing to clear the driveway when it snowed. The therapist she'd seen for a little while had helped her crawl out of this very dark depression, but when Rebecca had seen the therapist reading one of Victor Sutton's recent therapy books, she'd immediately ended their sessions.

Rebecca insisted they sit at the kitchen table with their pizzas. Lily even turned the television off. As Lily ate with a knife and fork, the rest of them ate with their hands and spoke about their lives. Chad and Shelby had a few more weeks of school left, after which Shelby planned to head to her job in the Acadia Mountains, where she would stay and work as a forest guide for hikers and campers. "Your father would be so proud of you," Rebecca said. Fred had scoured the Acadia Mountains with his children and taught them names of trees, flowers, and rocks. Around the time Shelby planned to leave, Chad had basketball camp in Virginia, which he'd attended every year since age twelve. Rebecca sensed he looked forward to it as a way of escapism. Fred's shadow loomed over all of them.

"What is this internship you have?" Shelby asked Lily.

"Oh, it's like social media and stuff," Lily described without explaining.

Shelby nodded as though she understood.

"Mom told me about the dinner thing at Bar Harbor

Brasserie?" Lily sounded doubtful. She had a forkful of pizza poised near her lips.

Shelby and Chad exchanged glances that told Rebecca they'd discussed this at length. Shelby softened her face.

"We're worried about you," she said to Rebecca.

Rebecca placed the rest of her slice back on the plate and wiped off her hands on a napkin. She felt like an exposed nerve. "I understand your concerns. I really do." She spoke like a businesswoman to a board of directors. "But you're all old enough to understand what I'm about to say."

Chad set his jaw, imitating an older man.

"Opening a restaurant is just about the most heinous thing you can do for yourself and your finances," Rebecca continued. "Your father was a cunning businessman, and he kept us in the black most of the time. Conveniently, the minute we closed in January, our rent went up. Not just a little bit, but a lot."

Lily's shoulders fell forward.

"As you know, we had a pop-up in the restaurant during the months of March and April, but the pop-up failed, and the owners have no interest in continuing the lease. I can't hold the restaurant space much longer, praying I'll be strong enough to reopen one day. I either have to bite the bullet and reopen, or..." Rebecca stalled. She did not want to say the truth out loud: that in order to keep herself and her children fed, clothed, and housed, she'd have to sell her and Fred's dream, pick up the pieces of her life, and maybe get work elsewhere. The fact that she hadn't so much as peeled a carrot since January was the least of her problems.

"Mindy Collins's idea for a big fundraiser dinner at

Bar Harbor Brasserie will buy us a bit of time," Rebecca continued. "It'll be like a test run. I've already told Dave about it, and he's in, as are several other servers and kitchen staff members. They've missed Bar Harbor Brasserie and want us to reopen. And maybe I owe them that. Perhaps I owe myself that."

Rebecca felt ridiculous. Her speech sounded straight out of a *Rocky* film. Unconvinced, her children glanced at one another and returned their attention to their pizza. Rebecca hurtled toward the remote control and turned the television back on. What had she been thinking when turning it off in the first place? She needed anything to eliminate the strain of their silences.

On the morning of the fundraiser dinner, Dave met Rebecca at the fish market at five forty-five in the morning. It was the end of May, and angry storm clouds floated in the early light. Dave hugged Rebecca warmly and handed her a cup of coffee. His emotions swayed easily, from eagerness to sorrow to excitement to fear.

Together, Rebecca and Dave had planned the four-course meal for the fundraiser. It featured clam chowder, pasta with a tart sardine sauce, Atlantic salmon, home-made bread, and a pear tart. Neighboring restaurants had contributed regional wines from their own cellars for the evening, grateful, they said, to be able to honor Fred and help his family.

Dave and Rebecca selected healthy-looking slabs of salmon, pounds of clams, and pounds of shining sardines. Little fish eyes glinted. Many vendors greeted Rebecca as family, asking her about Lily, Shelby, and Chad and saying they hoped to make it to the fundraiser later. "You've been an honored customer for years," one of them told her. "It's time for me to support you in return."

With three coolers loaded with fish, Rebecca and Dave drove downtown to prepare the kitchen. Rebecca had hired cleaners to fine-tune the place, and she'd even had Dave go early in the week to sharpen knives and ensure the ovens, stovetops, fridges, and freezers were in working order. He reported Bar Harbor Brasserie was as functional as ever. It just didn't have any working staff.

Outside the restaurant, Dave placed a hand on Rebecca's shoulder. "Do you want me to go in first?"

Rebecca's nostrils flared. When had she become so weak? Frozen, she stared at the back door of Bar Harbor Brasserie, one through which she'd come and gone thousands of times. She wasn't the first widow in the world. Women lost their husbands all the time.

"I can do it." Rebecca's keys jangled as she walked up to the door. Miraculously, the key turned, just as it always had, and she pressed herself into the familiar air of the back of the kitchen. Up ahead was her and Fred's office, and farther down the hallway, the door opened to the immaculate dining room. Her knees wiggled beneath her and threatened to drop her to the ground. "Okay," she told Dave. "Let's get started."

Oh. God. What had she been thinking? Even as she peeled potatoes as the first light of the morning streamed through the windows of the front of the restaurant, a part of her mind returned to easy avenues. It was instinct that made her think Fred was just in their office, doing payroll. It was instinct to think she needed to text Fred to pick up Shelby from school. She shook away her thoughts. After she'd peeled five pounds of potatoes, she stepped into the walk-in freezer, placed her hands over her face, and screamed until she cried. She'd done that back in culinary school when a soufflé had dropped, or she'd put too much seasoning or salt on a dish. *"The walk-in freezer is the ultimate therapy,"* a server had joked once. Rebecca had a hunch Victor Sutton had never included this fact in one of his top-selling books.

Staff members and lunchtime servers began to arrive at ten. The mood was celebratory, like a family coming back together again. The server who'd had the governor's table on the last day of Rebecca's life hugged Rebecca for a long time and announced she was pregnant. "But if you do reopen full-time, I'm prepared to work here until my baby doesn't let me anymore. Bar Harbor Brasserie is my family."

Rebecca congratulated and thanked her, even as a stone dropped into her stomach. Bar Harbor Brasserie had never been her family. Her family with Fred had been her family. *With Fred gone, did Bar Harbor Brasserie have validity anymore? Did it even matter?*

"Big day ahead, Chef!" A staffer waved as he passed with another bucket of potatoes.

Rebecca smiled at him and realized she no longer remembered his name. She felt as though she'd been planted in somebody else's kitchen. Could she even make clam chowder anymore? Could she perfect a pear tart?

Just before they opened for lunch at eleven, Mindy Collins stepped into the kitchen to say hello. Rebecca's voice brightened and became false.

"Mindy! This was your brainchild. Thank you for pushing us to reopen today."

Mindy showed all her teeth when she smiled. "You don't know how the restaurant scene has missed you."

"You don't know how I've missed it," Rebecca lied.

Mindy asked to understand the day's courses so she could discuss them with others later when she came for dinner. "I like to sound like I understand flavor pairings, even when I don't," she said. "It's all about research." Mindy had booked out most of the restaurant from seven thirty onward and promised that each table would bring in upward of one-hundred-and-fifty to two-hundred-dollar tabs. "We just want to help you and your family in any way we can. Our hope is you'll find a way to reopen before the summer season closes. We'd hate you to miss tourist season."

When Mindy left Rebecca in the kitchen, Rebecca wondered if Mindy wanted Bar Harbor Brasserie to reopen for Rebecca's sake or the tourists. Maybe both could be true. Perhaps Mindy wasn't a monster for wanting everything to be okay again.

The lunch rush was a doozy. Bar Harbor locals and old friends of Fred's stopped to feast and day drink. Over their second glasses of Cabernet, they demanded their servers track down Rebecca so they could say hello. *"She is one of our oldest and dearest friends."* Often when Rebecca appeared at the table, she couldn't remember their names, either. *Was grief the reason for this?* In the kitchen, she googled "losing your memory and grief," and too many sites popped up at once. She put her phone back in her pocket.

At seven thirty, Mindy and her high-rolling friends arrived for the feast. Even from the kitchen, Rebecca could smell the weight of their expensive colognes—she could feel the existence of their yachts, which floated in Frenchman Bay. Begrudgingly, she washed her hands and styled her hair and stepped into the dining room to greet them, barely holding it together when they complimented her restaurant and said how sorry they were about Fred.

Restaurants like hers and Fred's made Bar Harbor culturally interesting. For this reason, restaurants like hers and Fred's lined the pockets of the upper echelon of Bar Harbor's locals—these people who now sat at her tables and spoke about recent trips to Tuscany and how difficult it was to hire hardworking staff at their luxury hotels.

Rebecca struggled to breathe. For the fourth time that day, she stepped into the walk-in freezer and allowed herself a full minute to cry. When she returned to the frenetic chaos of her kitchen, she heard herself bark out the orders on a printing ticket and demand that first courses be plated. During these moments, delirium fell over her, and she was no longer sure what year it was or how old her children were. She just had to find a way to survive the night.

Out of nowhere, it was ten. Dave came over to hug her and congratulate her on the success of the day. Rebecca hugged him back with arms like cotton. She hadn't eaten so much as a cracker in over twelve hours.

Suddenly, Mindy was back in the kitchen, showing all her teeth. She thanked Rebecca twice and squeezed her upper arm. "Oh, darling, you really have gotten too skinny." She allowed her face a moment of pity for the widow before her, then returned to her smile. "The folks out front would really love to hear from you. I don't suppose you could grace us with your presence and put in a little face time?"

Mindy hinted it was appropriate, given that all these people had come out to support Rebecca and wanted so desperately to keep her in business. Rebecca removed her hairnet and checked her face in the mirror. She didn't recognize it as her own, but it was the only one she had, so it would have to do.

Out in the dining room, plates had been cleared, wine had been refilled, and Mindy's rich pals rejoiced, laughing easily and speaking conspiratorially, perhaps about all the delicious money they would make together. Rebecca had never felt more lost. She followed Mindy through her own restaurant, shook hands with her friends, and thanked them for their support. At each table, they told her just how talented she was and that she shouldn't hide her talent away. "Bar Harbor needs a restaurant like Bar Harbor Brasserie. Please, let us know how we can help you reopen." By the sixth or seventh table, Rebecca wasn't sure she wouldn't collapse.

If only Fred was there. If only he could put on his friendly and easy smile and chat the hours away with these people in a way that would lead them to leave business cards and invite him to golf outings he would eventually decline. No, he hadn't been like these people—far from it, but he'd understood how to play their game in ways Rebecca had not, which was essential in any world but especially in hospitality and tourism.

Just when Rebecca planned to bolt back into the kitchen and hide herself in the freezer until the storm had passed, she turned to find a single man at a corner table, watching her. Mindy hadn't introduced them, but perhaps, in Mindy's world, he wasn't important. But something about his eyes caught Rebecca off guard. Watching her watch him, he nodded. The twinkle in his eye sent a shiver of distaste up her spine.

And suddenly, she bolted to him. He remained just as he was, his hands clasped beneath his bearded chin, his eyes falsely compassionate. Rebecca kept an icy smile glued to her face. It occurred to her this might be a dream. When she reached his table, she bent down and hissed with as much vitriol as she could muster, "What the are you doing here?"

After that, she collapsed.

Chapter Three

Rebecca wasn't out long. She blinked at her hands on the hardwood and listened to the steady rhythm of conversations. "Property value" and "Yale" and "the Hamptons" were discussed, as was the probability of the euro's value falling even lower. Nobody noticed the forty-something woman on the ground. Nobody except the man she'd tumbled in front of, that is.

Victor Sutton leaned down from his chair. "Are you all right, Rebecca?"

Rebecca lifted her chin to stare into his eyes. They were as hard as steel, an icy blue. *How could anyone peer into them and find solace?* He was the great family psychologist Victor Sutton, but his eyes told the truth of who he was—a villain.

"I asked you what you're doing here." Rebecca's voice wavered. She clung to the edge of his table and heaved herself to her feet. A passing server hustled over to help, but Rebecca waved her off.

"I'm here for the same reason all these people are

here. To eat," her father said. "It was remarkable, by the way. The salmon was seasoned to perfection. And that sardine pasta sauce! I haven't had anything like it in my life."

Unfortunately, Rebecca wasn't immune to her father's praise. It was as though he'd just complimented her crayon drawing or an A on a math test. She studied his face, which was still remarkably handsome this close to seventy. The beard, which he'd worn since his twenties, gave him an academic charm, one that probably assisted him in his career. Talk show hosts wouldn't dream of featuring psychologists without appropriate Freud-like beards.

"Bar Harbor is a long way from Providence."

Her father smiled. "It is, isn't it? It looks so much closer on the map."

Rebecca wasn't in the mood to laugh.

"Why don't you sit with me? Have a drink? It looks as though all your guests have been served."

Rebecca scanned the tables. Candlelight flickered menacingly over the guests' faces. Her gut told her to go into the back, find Fred in the office, and take off for the Florida Keys. "My father's back. He wants something. I just know it." But Rebecca couldn't listen to her gut anymore. It lied constantly.

"Not here." Rebecca's voice made her sound on the brink of a nervous breakdown. Maybe she was.

"Anywhere you'd like."

Rebecca pushed the swinging door open to return to the warm pulse of the kitchen. Staff members cleaned the stovetops and the ovens and chatted about their after-work plans. A few noticed her smile as she walked in, as though her presence gave them a grounding she couldn't

30

understand. How she wished she could reopen Bar Harbor Brasserie for them and return to a life that made sense.

Rebecca rapped on the countertop to make a final announcement. She thanked them for their honest service, for their ability to bring such remarkable energy to Bar Harbor Brasserie. She thanked them for being her support during a particularly dark time. And then, before she could chicken out, she revealed she would not reopen Bar Harbor Brasserie. Her heart couldn't take it. It was still with Fred, wherever he had gone.

With her jacket on, Rebecca walked out the back door, scooted around the restaurant, and discovered her father already outside. He wore a long trench coat and a hat that reminded her of spy novels. She stopped short and studied him, her mouth dry and her stomach gurgling with angry hunger.

After a period of silence that stretched far too long, Victor said, "I'll explain when we sit down. Where can we get a drink around here? By the looks of it, you need one. Bad."

Two streets away from Bar Harbor Brasserie was a hole-in-the-wall bar called Baxter's. Rebecca hadn't been there often, just a handful of times with previous employees. Her favorite bar was two streets from Bar Harbor Brasserie in the opposite direction, but she couldn't go there. It was yet another minefield in a town of minefields. She and Fred had collapsed there for after-work drinks more times than she could count.

Baxter's wasn't exactly the sort of bar you took prestigious family psychologist Victor Sutton to. At the counter, Rebecca removed her jacket and collapsed on a stool as Victor studied the graffiti on the walls and the hot dogs that rotated on sticks near the window. Baxter himself had told Rebecca the hot dogs were a way to lure drunk customers in to buy more beer.

Baxter wasn't working that night, but his brother was. He poured Rebecca and Victor hefty pints and knew not to ask Rebecca questions about her night. Rebecca ordered a grilled cheese sandwich, which she knew they cooked in a half-clean sandwich maker in the back. Nobody had died of food poisoning yet.

Victor raised his pint glass and studied Rebecca. Rebecca felt on display. "I feel like we should toast to something."

Rebecca took a long sip of her beer. Victor didn't bother to shield his disappointment.

"How did you know we were open tonight?" Rebecca said under her breath. She was barely audible over the loudspeaker, which played rock from the seventies and eighties.

Victor leaned toward her. "What?"

"Why did you show up tonight?" Rebecca demanded again. Rage bubbled through her stomach.

"I read about it," Victor explained. "There was an article about tonight's dinner in a magazine at my dentist office in Providence. Something about the entire Bar Harbor hospitality community coming together to support you. It was heartwarming, to say the least."

Rebecca raised an eyebrow. "That seems unlikely."

"Bar Harbor Brasserie is an iconic restaurant in Bar Harbor. People have heard of it. Even my dental hygienist has."

Rebecca wasn't sure if she wanted to believe anything he said. At his core, he was a liar—the sort of liar who knew to say just enough of the truth to get away with anything. Perhaps he'd been stalking her online for a while, waiting for the right time to pounce. If so, that begged the question: why? What did he want from her? What did Rebecca Vance have to give a man who had everything? Her respect? Her love? She didn't have any of that left for him.

"So. Okay." Rebecca sipped her beer. "That means you've known about my restaurant for a while."

"The internet is a remarkable place. You can discover just about anything on there."

So he had been stalking her. He knew about her career and her children. He knew about Fred's death. He knew she struggled with money. What did Rebecca know of Victor? She'd tried hard to leech him from her life like poison from a snake bite.

"It was brave of you to reopen tonight," her father said.

Rebecca turned to look at him too quickly, causing her neck to shimmer with pain. "It wasn't brave."

"It was. Everyone there knows what you've gone through. They all know you've had the worst few months of your life. There's no hiding from them, not when you're the one preparing their food. Not when you're the one they're paying."

Rebecca tried to focus on her breathing, but she felt too erratic. "I don't need a psychologist to explain to me why tonight was difficult."

"I know. You've never needed anyone. You made that very clear when you were a little girl."

Rebecca hadn't seen anyone from her childhood since she'd left Nantucket. Nobody had the authority to speak about her life pre-Bar Harbor, not even Fred. She drank her beer and studied the wall in front of them. Shelves bent under the weight of Jack Daniel's and Gordon's gin bottles. Baxter's brother sang the lyrics to a Billy Joel song that wasn't on the stereo.

It seemed clear to Victor that Rebecca wasn't eager to speak. He drank his beer as well, waiting for something. Perhaps Rebecca could sit and ignore him till he got the hint to walk out the door and never find her again.

But after another five minutes of silence, Rebecca said, "You would have liked him. Everyone liked him."

Victor didn't respond right away. Rebecca turned and glared at him, swimming in sorrow.

"He never would have walked out on his family like that," Rebecca continued.

Victor's face didn't reveal any emotion. Perhaps he'd never felt any guilt for what he'd done. "I'm sure he wouldn't have," he said.

Rebecca sniffed. "He was a remarkable man, and I loved him. I loved him so much more than I even understood. Like, I wish I would have explained it to him. That my love was different from other kinds of love."

Why was she blabbering on and on to the father who'd abandoned her? Had she lost her mind? Worst of all, he probably took pleasure in this. This was his livelihood, after all. He was Dr. Sutton, famous psychologist.

"Go ahead. Analyze me," Rebecca said. "I can take it."

But instead, he shook his head. "He knew you loved him that much. We humans always know. And sometimes we experience emotions that have no language."

Rebecca returned her attention to her beer. She hated how right he was; she hated more that she liked the sentiment. Still, she couldn't let him in. She wouldn't. There wasn't a single thing he could do or say to mend the decades-worth of silence and heartache. Nothing he could do would change her mind about who he was and what he'd done.

"Your mother's husband died."

The words landed like a bomb. Rebecca turned and gaped at him, shocked. "Larry died?"

Victor nodded. "Two weeks ago."

Rebecca placed her hand over her mouth. Although she'd never met her mother's second husband, she'd seen photographs online that marked him as a literary type, with thick, horn-rimmed glasses and a perpetually loving gaze. Finally, her mother had found peace. Finally, she'd found the one.

"He was so young," Rebecca breathed. "What happened?"

"Heart attack," Victor said. "Out of nowhere."

Rebecca stared at her empty glass. Lately, life seemed eager to sneak up and remind her of all the possible ways to die. "Poor Mom."

"Yes." Victor palmed the back of his neck. "A source back in Nantucket says she's not doing too well."

Rebecca's ears perked up. "Your brother?"

Victor nodded. "I've been back a few times over the years to see them."

"Did you see Mom?" She asked it too quickly, like a child.

Victor shook her head. "I drove by the Book Club. It looked as beautiful as ever. Your mother and Larry added another back garden and planted several trees."

Rebecca's heart cracked at the edges. She imagined her beautiful mother knee-deep in soil, tending to a vegetable garden as her husband, Larry, mowed the lawn.

It was domesticity at its finest; it was consistent proof of your love and your will to tend it.

"I hate thinking of her alone in that big house," Rebecca breathed. Already, she'd begun to imagine herself alone in that big, drafty house when Chad moved out. It was a house that had once echoed with laughter and children's arguments and Fred's deep, baritone singing voice. She would walk through it like a ghost.

"Me too," Victor said.

Rebecca met his gaze, genuinely confused. *Why did Victor Sutton care if Esme was alone in her big house back in Nantucket?* Why had he traveled such a long distance to tell Rebecca any of this?

Finally, he slowly dredged the truth to the surface. "I find myself without a home these days."

Rebecca's lips parted with surprise.

"It's not that I can't afford one. I could very well buy another in Providence, Bar Harbor, or Timbuktu."

Rebecca felt a wave of annoyance pass over her. She hated his braggadocios baloney.

"But the issue, I suppose, is that I'm getting divorced again." Victor's eyes were empty and wide. "And I find myself, if not an old man, then an aging man with plenty of questions about my past and my roots. This is why I've come to you, Rebecca. I want you to accompany me to Nantucket. I want you to come with me to visit your mother. I want us to return to the place where everything fell apart."

Rebecca's ears were ringing. Baxter's brother collected their pint glasses and refilled them without asking, as though this was the bar culture at Baxter's.

"I don't know what to say," Rebecca whispered.

"Say you'll think about it."

Rebecca bristled. But when she turned to look at her father again, she saw what she hadn't seen before. Here was a man who was broken. His suit jacket slumped from his shoulders, as though he'd lost a bit of weight and no longer fit into his academic clothes. His eyes were moist and tinged with red. Then there was the fact that he'd traveled from Providence to Bar Harbor to see his daughter for the first time in thirty years—which was no easy feat. The Victor Sutton who'd left them on Nantucket wouldn't have stooped this low.

"Don't you want to make sure your mother is okay?" Victor rasped.

Rebecca wanted to push back at that. She wanted to ask how he could use Esme's grief to manipulate her.

Then again, fear about her mother's mental health had begun to shadow everything else. Since January, Rebecca had had to keep everything at least marginally together for the sake of her children. But in that big house alone, Esme didn't have anything to prove.

"We don't have to stay for long," Victor urged. "Just a day or two. Just enough time for us to sit with Esme and make sure she'll get through this."

Rebecca closed her eyes. On the stereo, a commercial advertised brand-new mattresses and their owners' desire to remain in bed all day long.

"I can't go until Chad is off to basketball camp and Shelby's in the mountains for work." Rebecca closed her eyes and rubbed her temples.

"I understand," her father said. "And your eldest?"

"She has an internship," Rebecca said. "She's an adult. I don't need to worry about her as much anymore."

Her father quieted for a moment. Rebecca opened

her eyes to peer at him. He studied the top rim of his beer glass like a scientist.

"What are you thinking?" Rebecca demanded.

After a pause, he answered. "You say you don't need to worry about your eldest as much anymore. But that's just not true, is it? We always worry about our children, no matter how much time has passed, and no matter how old they are."

Chapter Four

The Acadia Mountains and Bar Harbor's sea level boasted a twenty-five-degree difference. Rebecca shivered in her spring jacket as she lugged Shelby's second suitcase from the back of the SUV and followed her into the cabin she would share with the other employees for the summer. By the time she swung the bag onto Shelby's upper bunk, Shelby was in conversation with a young woman from Sweden who'd traveled all this way for the American experience. "Do you know anything about s'mores?" the woman asked Shelby, who laughed and told her she was in for a treat.

This was the final goodbye of a week of goodbyes. Rebecca perched at the edge of Shelby's bed and swung her feet in front of her. Yesterday, she'd taken Chad to the airport with three of his basketball friends for their flight to Virginia. Although she'd hugged the other boys goodbye, she'd clung to Chad a bit too long. The other boys had exchanged worried glances. Their parents had probably spoken about Rebecca, the new widow, and told their children to be extra kind to Chad.

Three days ago, Rebecca had taken Lily back to New York City for her paid internship in marketing. Lily had taken a sublease in Brooklyn and said she was grateful to be out of Columbia's shadow for a little while. Come fall, she would enter her final year at the estimable university, a fact that boggled Rebecca's mind. What was next? Neither Rebecca nor Lily was eager to find out.

"Are you going to be okay by yourself?" Shelby asked her mother as she walked her out to the SUV.

"I'll be fine, sweetie. You know me."

"I do." Shelby furrowed her brow. A large eagle swept overhead. "I think it's a good thing you decided to sell the restaurant."

Rebecca dropped her gaze. "I couldn't believe how quickly it became a bidding war."

"It's a great location," Shelby pointed out.

"I just hope it isn't an Asian fusion restaurant. Or, ugh, another Italian place. Or a silly coffee shop that only sells sugary foods."

"Whatever it is, it won't be as good as Bar Harbor Brasserie. Everyone knows that."

Shelby adjusted the straps of her tank top. Rebecca was pretty sure Lily had passed this particular one down to her. It reminded Rebecca of her own sisters, with whom she'd continually swapped clothes with. *What would her sisters have said about Victor Sutton reappearing in her life out of the blue? Why hadn't she asked her father if they'd been in contact?*

Rebecca hadn't told her children about Victor Sutton or her Nantucket plans. She was terrified about what they would say. *Mom, have you gone insane? Mom, you swore you'd never see your father again. Mom, what's gotten into you?* Although she owed them the truth in all things, she simply hadn't gotten around to figuring out the best way to explain her motivations. She wasn't entirely sure what those were herself.

Rebecca sobbed all the way down the mountain. She hated how her children worried about her. She hated everyone's pity. But most of all, she cried with terror about the approaching trip to Nantucket. *What could she say to her mother after so many years away?*

Esme had been just as quiet as Rebecca. She hadn't invited Rebecca to Nantucket. She hadn't told her about her marriage. She'd never met Rebecca's children.

Still, Rebecca was plagued with guilt. Now that she was a mother, she ached with fear that her children would one day turn their back on her. To Esme, it must have felt like a death sentence.

* * *

Victor Sutton waited for Rebecca outside the hotel on the edge of town. It was early, but he looked well-slept, agile, and cool in a pair of jeans, a suit jacket, and a pair of sunglasses. As he swung his suitcase into the back of the SUV, he whistled and said, "Good morning, Rebecca."

Rebecca smiled as her father got into the passenger seat. Behind her own sunglasses, half-moons hung beneath her eyes. She hadn't slept well in the big, empty house and spent hours tossing and turning.

"You'll let me know when you want to switch seats?" Victor asked.

"Sure." Rebecca eased from the hotel and toward the highway that would take them south to Nantucket. She felt out of her mind. "How was the hotel?"

"Not bad," Victor reported. "They had a pretty good

41

breakfast. Eggs, bacon, pancakes, and even some fresh fruit. The good stuff, too. Strawberries, raspberries, and blueberries."

"No melon?"

"No melon. Thank goodness. What a waste of time that fruit is."

Rebecca chuckled. She couldn't believe she'd remembered her father's distaste for melon.

During the first hour or so, Rebecca and Victor chatted easily, like two strangers on a road trip. Victor had spent two weeks in Bar Harbor as Rebecca had gotten her children ready for their summer, which Rebecca was curious about. *What had Victor gotten up to?* Victor reported having eaten his weight in lobster. He'd gotten caught up on some reading and taken some long walks. He didn't press her about not having allowed him to meet her children. When he'd asked once via text message, she'd said, "Let me think about it," and neither of them had brought it up again.

As they drove, Rebecca again had the impression her father was much different than he used to be. *Was it possible that a couple of decades had softened him? Was it possible he was a world-renowned family psychologist for a reason?*

It was almost a seven-hour journey to Hyannis Port and the longest road trip Rebecca had planned since Fred's and her honeymoon. Back then, they'd driven from Denver to Los Angeles, running up and down mountain ranges in a car that shouldn't have been able to handle the terrain. They'd made it to LA "on a wing and a prayer," or so Fred had said.

After two hours, Victor drove for a little while. He had his hands at nine and three, and he asked questions about Rebecca's children in a way that almost made her regret not allowing him to meet them.

"Shelby's my responsible child. She overthinks everything," Rebecca explained. "And Chad's Mr. Congeniality. He has more friends than I've ever had in my life. Oh, and Lily." She paused with worry for her eldest, all alone in Brooklyn. "She's my creative child. She has moments of pure sadness and depression. Fred and I did our best to support her artistic pursuits."

"That's healthy for a child with so many complicated emotions," her father said firmly with all the authority of a child psychologist. "You and Fred were right to do that."

Rebecca eyed her father. A part of her wanted to ask him how he could present himself to the world as an esteemed psychologist. *Didn't he remember their past?* But another part of her felt oddly proud that her father respected her parenting skills.

"I didn't tell them about our trip to Nantucket," Rebecca explained. "I didn't want to worry them."

"They've gone through a lot this year," Victor affirmed. "And as their mother, you have to trust your instincts."

Rebecca blushed, sensing her father's pride. He was right. She had to trust herself because she was all she had left now.

Halfway to Hyannis, Rebecca and Victor stopped for lunch at a diner. Attached to a gas station, the diner brought in truckers and road trippers and families on their way someplace else. Rebecca and Victor stretched their legs around the parking lot and warmed their faces beneath the early June sun.

"Remember when we drove to Florida?" Victor asked. They turned toward the front door of the diner.

"Barely. I must have been seven."

Victor eyed her, his smile faltering. "You and Bethany fought the entire way."

Rebecca bristled at her sister's name. She pushed open the diner door, and a bell jangled overhead.

"Your mother had it up to here," Victor continued, gesturing around his ear. "We got out of the car somewhere in South Carolina, and she demanded you and Bethany explain what was wrong."

"Huh." Rebecca scanned the heads of diners, careful to appear apathetic. A server approached, adjusting her apron around her hips.

"Turns out, Bethany thought you'd stolen her doll, and you'd thought she'd stolen your doll. But you'd accidentally switched dolls when you'd fallen asleep and were too tired to figure that out." Victor's laughter turned his cheeks bright red.

"Two?" The server handed Rebecca two menus and beckoned for Rebecca and Victor to follow her to a booth. There, Rebecca slid onto the vinyl cushion and stared at the menu as her father adjusted across from her.

The story about Bethany had made Rebecca jittery. *Why had her father brought it up? Did he want to remind her of how normal their family had once been before he'd abandoned them during their darkest hour? Did he want to call attention to the elephant in the room? Was he that ignorant?*

The blurry menu contained photographs of midgrade breakfast and lunch items such as waffles, chicken tenders, and grilled cheese sandwiches.

"I'll have the three-bean soup," Victor said, "and a turkey club." He passed the menu to the server, who glanced at Rebecca.

"And I'll just have a chicken salad with the dressing on the side." Since nothing tasted good to Rebecca anymore, it was best to stick to the basics.

"Anything to drink?"

Both Rebecca and her father ordered water. Rebecca stared out the window for a full minute as Victor checked something on his cell phone. After he finished, he waved his cell in the air and said, "Pretty wild how far technology has come over the years, huh?"

Rebecca had the sudden urge to run out of the diner and away from this man as quickly and as far as she could.

When the food came, Victor scooped a large portion of bean soup and blew over it. Rebecca shifted her fork through her salad.

"So. What happened?" Rebecca lifted her eyes to his.

Victor chewed and swallowed his spoonful of soup. "What do you mean?"

Rebecca shrugged. "With Bree."

Victor's eyes became shadowed. He took another bite of bean soup.

"I mean, she was the love of your life. Right?" Rebecca hated that she suddenly sounded a little bit like Lily during an argument.

Victor set his jaw. "You were married for many years. You know how complicated it is."

"My marriage was a success," Rebecca retorted. "We were loyal to each other. We held each other's love above everything else."

Victor blinked at her. Rebecca's cheeks burned with shame.

"As a family psychologist, I've seen hundreds, if not thousands, of couples," Victor recited. "And I..."

"Oh, don't give me your 'I'm a family psychologist' crap."

Victor couldn't look at her. Rebecca took a breath and told herself to calm down.

"I don't necessarily think my marriage to Bree was unsuccessful," Victor said softly. "We were married for thirty years and built an entire life together. There's a quote from John Updike that I love. 'If temporality is held to be invalidating, then nothing real succeeds.' I suppose, to me, it means that nothing in life is meant to last forever. But that doesn't mean we shouldn't honor what we've had."

Rebecca sipped her water. She felt on the verge of bursting into tears. The only thing that stopped her was her sheer embarrassment of crying in front of world-renowned family psychologist Victor Sutton, especially in a public place.

"I just don't think you have any right to tell anyone how to live their lives when you've had so much trouble with yours," Rebecca muttered. She then leaped to her feet and hustled into the women's bathroom. She collapsed on the toilet lid and wept into her hands, feeling like a child.

Rebecca remained in the bathroom for fifteen minutes. A part of her thought Victor had taken off in her SUV by now. But no, there he sat in front of a paper to-go box, in which he'd placed the rest of his sandwich and an additional turkey club he'd had made just for her.

"You might be hungry later." He spoke to the box rather than her.

Outside, Rebecca got into the driver's seat and turned the engine on. For a long time, they sat in silence.

"I'm sorry I asked about Bree," Rebecca said.

"It's okay." Victor palmed the back of his neck. "I have so many things to apologize for."

Rebecca waited for him to explain which things, but he didn't. *When would those apologies come?*

"Have you reached out to Bethany or Valerie?" Rebecca asked. She didn't dare look at her father.

"No."

"Why not? Don't you think they'd want to know about Mom?"

Victor shrugged. "I'm sure they would."

Rebecca's ego felt bruised. As she backed the SUV out of the parking lot, she dared herself to face the truth. She felt the weakest and more accessible of the three Sutton sisters. Hers was the life farthest from the tracks. Therefore, Victor Sutton had come to pluck her up, perhaps as collateral to ensure Esme would see him again.

But with nowhere else to go and nothing else to do, Rebecca could do nothing but keep driving. Hyannis Port was a little more than three hours away.

Chapter Five

It was difficult for Ben Roberts to remember everything that had happened since 9/11. Like every other American, the event had terrified him so much that he'd sat on the couch for what felt like many weeks, holding his new wife, Terry, and wondering how everything in the world had gone so wrong. Unlike many other Americans, Ben had decided to do something about it. He'd dropped out of his college courses and enlisted in the Army with plans to go overseas. Terry had begged him not to go; she'd never signed up to be an Army wife. But Ben had told her he'd finally found his purpose. It wasn't accounting, and it wasn't landscape work. It was to fight for his country, just as others had before him.

What happened to Ben happened to thousands upon thousands of other men in Afghanistan and Iraq. Their first tour ripped them apart, either metaphorically or literally. Ben was one of the luckier ones, as his destruction was metaphorical. But when he returned to Terry's warm embrace, she found he was no longer the Ben she'd once fallen in love with. He hardly slept. He paced the living room, muttering to himself, and looked at her as though she was a stranger. When the Army came crawling back to ask him for another tour, Terry served him divorce papers. She couldn't do this anymore. She couldn't wait around as he fought to destroy himself.

Ben completed four tours overseas. His fifth ended with a gunshot wound through the arm. He'd retired with honors and returned to a country he no longer recognized. He'd been overseas too long and given too much of himself to the cause. Maybe there was nothing left to salvage.

It was now nearly twenty-two years after 9/11 and ten years after his last tour. Due to the ever-weaving nature of life and a few lucky breaks, he'd found his way to Nantucket Island, a place prettier than any daydream. What had begun as a temporary vacation had extended for five years at this point. Anyone who asked him why he stayed so long just didn't get it. It wasn't like he had anywhere else to go.

Besides, Doug was on Nantucket. Doug was the only person who'd ever needed Ben. And Ben needed Doug just as much, if not more.

About six months into his stay on Nantucket, Ben had spotted a pamphlet. It read **"Free Dinner for Veterans @ the Sutton Book Club."** Intrigued, Ben had left his part-time job early that night to shower in his ramshackle apartment and walk over.

Much like many other veterans, Ben had never had a lot of money. He'd never graduated from college, and he had a bad arm. His PTSD could be so debilitating that he had to take weeks off work, which wasn't easy to explain to employers. On Nantucket, he'd bounced from washing dishes to serving at restaurants to loading the freights that brought food and beverages from the mainland. No matter where he worked, he always stuck out like a sore thumb. He was sunken-eyed and exhausted. His hair was unkempt, and his face, though handsome, seemed to echo the tragedies he'd seen.

On the night of the veterans' dinner, the Sutton Book Club wasn't an unknown to Ben. He'd passed the old colonial hundreds of times since his arrival to Nantucket. It was white with pillars, a long porch with a swing, and black shutters, and it demanded respect for reasons beyond its beauty. Ben had just never imagined he'd have an invitation to go in.

That first evening at the Sutton Book Club, Ben walked in the front door to the musty scent of books filling his nostrils. A sense of calm washed over his body as he looked around at the towering walls. Rows upon rows of bookshelves brimmed with the promise of new worlds and knowledge. The colorful array of books bore the titles of non-fiction, classic, and contemporary tales on their spines.

The warm glow of the overhead lamps on each table offered the perfect ambience for reading. The sturdy and smooth tables provided a comfortable surface for people to rest their books on. As he looked around, he couldn't help but notice the cozy couches placed strategically around the room, inviting patrons to sit and relax while they read.

As he made his way through the library, he couldn't help but be drawn to the long sat counter, with an open entrance to the side leading to a mysterious back room. As he passed through the threshold, the scene before him was one of lively chatter and camaraderie. Veterans filled the long rows of tables, each one lost in conversation and reminiscing about their past experiences over steaming cups of coffee. He watched as they all chatted, laughed, and sipped their drinks, their eyes wide and skittish, and their limbs and faces presented a patchwork of scars. It seemed they represented every war, going as far back as World War II. A sense of warmth and community filled the room, so Ben couldn't help but feel a sense of belonging as he took a seat among them.

Ben had sat across from two other men who'd been in Afghanistan. They seemed chummy. One of them got up to refill his coffee while the other asked where Ben had been stationed. He explained where he'd been and cracked open his can of iced tea. The smell of spices hung heavy in the air, presumably from whatever was cooking in another back room off to the side that he assumed was a kitchen. Ben's stomach gurgled. It had been a long time since he'd had a good meal.

One of the oldest men Ben had ever seen sat at the far end of the table. His wrinkles folded onto one another, cascading like a waterfall down his face. His shoulders remained wide, and he seemed to have use of his legs, although he fiddled with a cane to the right of his chair. As the guy who'd gotten Ben a beer passed the older man, he patted his shoulder and said, "How's it hanging, Dougie?"

The older man snarled. "I've told you time and again. My name is not Dougie."

Ben stifled a laugh. Both men who'd gone to Afghanistan exchanged glances as though they couldn't understand why Doug deserved the respect he demanded. But Ben, who hadn't felt an ounce of respect since the day he'd signed up to go overseas, saw a soul mate in Doug. All he had to do was find a way to get close to him. All he had to do was show Doug how much he needed a friend.

That night, Ben had learned about the grand history of the Sutton Book Club's Veterans' Night. Just as she always did, Esme had told the story of her father, Thomas, who'd served in World War II before his return to Nantucket. At that time, he'd begun to collect books— everything from antiques to paperbacks—and he'd eventually founded the Sutton Book Club. Because he was a veteran and understood the horrors his brethren had faced, he'd begun Veterans' Night as a way to draw Nantucket veterans together. The support had extended far past his death. Esme spoke of it as a necessity. It was a way to help her father's tradition live on.

It was now four and a half years since that fateful night. Ben stood in the kitchen of the shoddy house he rented, which was perpetually on the brink of falling apart against the wear and tear of the sea air. Out the window, he could just make out Doug's knees, where he sat on the front porch and smoked his pipe. For the first year or so after Ben and Doug had become real friends, Ben had asked Doug to quit the pipe. *"What good is it doing you?"* But now that Doug was ninety-eight years old and still going strong, Ben had decided to stop the nagging. The man could do what he wanted. It was his life. And he'd already done pretty good for himself. After all, not everyone lived to ninety-eight. Not everyone was stubborn enough to.

"How are you feeling?" Ben stepped into the June sunlight on the front porch and leaned against the railing.

Doug pulled the pipe from his lips. "You better not lean on that. It might be the only thing keeping this house standing."

Ben laughed, then shifted his weight forward. "You want me to make you some tea?" Doug didn't like to admit how sick he'd been lately. The chilly spring weather had seeped into the house and affected his sleep, resulting in a horrible cough.

"I'm tired of tea," Doug confessed. "I want a beer."

Ben saluted him. "You know what? You're right. It's five thirty. I'd say that's beer o'clock."

Ben collected two Buds from the fridge and returned to the porch, where he sat next to Doug and peered out along the soft sands of a quiet Nantucket beach. The house itself had been passed down from Doug's father, who'd died more than forty years ago. It wasn't lost on Ben that Doug's father had been dead almost as long as Ben had been alive.

It hadn't been Doug's idea for Ben to move in; it hadn't really been Ben's, either. It had just sort of happened, like so many other things in life. Ben and Doug had developed a lovely rapport with one another, one that the other veterans at the Sutton Book Club had noticed at their dinners. One evening, Doug had not been present, and Ben had felt listless and panicked, worrying about Doug's whereabouts. *Did anyone check on him?*

Esme Gardner, the owner and organizer of the Sutton Book Club, had noticed Ben's concern. She'd cornered him in the hallway and said that Doug had suffered a minor stroke, one he would probably fully recover from. Ben had nearly fallen to the floor. *"Where is he?"* he'd demanded. He'd gone to the hospital immediately and sat next to Doug's bed, anxious to hear him laugh. Doug had made fun of Ben's anxiety. *"I'm an old man. Just let me have a stroke and be done with it."*

But Doug needed someone at home to help him. In the wake of his stroke, walking had been challenging for him. Ben had teased him gently and kept his spirits up. And between his jokes, he'd managed to cook and clean.

Toward the end of Doug's healing journey, he'd spat sunflower seeds off the porch and grunted, "Where is it you live, anyway?"

Ben had told him he lived in a crummy apartment building on the outskirts of town.

"No view of the water?" Doug had demanded.

"No. I can't afford that."

Doug had grunted again. "That won't do at all."

Ben had gotten the hint. Being a man from his generation, he couldn't say what he wanted aloud, but Doug wanted Ben to stay. More than that, he needed him to.

Now that Doug was more or less over his recent illness, Ben and Doug decided to head to the Sutton Book Club for dinner. They'd missed the past two events the week previous, as they'd sequestered themselves off from the world, careful about Doug's intolerance for new germs and Ben's intolerance for people who weren't Doug.

Ben never worried about the fact that his only friend in the world was a ninety-eight-year-old man. He knew loneliness would come for him one of these days. But he chose to enjoy their time together rather than worry and regret.

Ben drove them to the Sutton Book Club in Doug's ancient, clunky pickup truck. Doug hadn't driven in a few years, although Ben was careful not to insinuate that Doug couldn't do it.

"I hope Esme makes her chicken tonight," Doug said.

He had his cane between his legs and clutched the handle thoughtfully.

"I love that brisket she makes," Ben said.

"The chicken is miles better than the brisket," Doug insisted.

The route to the Sutton Book Club was a doozy. Over the span of Doug's illness, tourists had returned to the island in full force, and the population had doubled or tripled. The nice weather and gorgeous sunshine distracted the tourists, and they rushed across intersections and kept no tabs on approaching traffic.

"Dang tourists. They always come here and act like they own the place," Doug spat.

Ben laughed. "I don't think Nantucket could survive without them."

"We could," Doug insisted, although Ben knew that wasn't true. The only income he ever brought in came from odd jobs here and there, all of which were hospitality-based. The money he and Doug got from the government was abysmal. It couldn't have kept a donkey alive.

Ben parked Doug's truck in one of the handicapped parking spaces directly in front of the Sutton Book Club. Esme had had the spots set up specially for the veterans who came to Veterans' Night. This was just another reason she was a godsend—one of the most caring and loving individuals Ben had ever met. Because Ben's mother had died when he was fifteen, he often wondered if he thought of Esme as a motherly figure. She certainly watched out for him, just as she watched out for all of them.

Ben popped out of the driver's side. Doug cracked his passenger door, as well, never willing to let Ben help him out unless he felt particularly weak. To avoid unnecessary accidents, Ben stepped casually around to Doug's side and monitored the situation. All the while, he kept one eye on the front porch of the Sutton House, where two people he'd never seen before stood and peered through the windows.

"Do you know those folks?" Ben asked Doug.

Doug took a step forward with his cane. "I don't think so."

"Why are they staring in the windows? Isn't it open?" Ben and Doug walked slowly down the sidewalk and up the walkway to the main entrance. As they got closer, Ben analyzed the man and woman on the front porch—and was soon able to hear them bickering.

"Why is it closed, Dad?" the woman muttered. She was a good deal younger than her father, perhaps in her forties, with dark hair curling past her shoulders and an athletic build that she'd dressed in a floral summer dress.

"How would I know?" her father demanded. He was maybe in his late sixties or early seventies, and he wore a sleek suit jacket and a pair of jeans. He had an air of importance about him while his daughter's shoulders rounded forward as though defeated.

"Excuse me?" Ben asked from below the porch steps.

The woman and her father turned to frown down at Ben and Doug. They looked at them as though they didn't belong.

"Hi," the woman said. She looked exhausted, and her eyes were bloodshot. "Do you have any idea why it's closed?"

Doug and Ben exchanged worried glances. Ben said, "We're here for Veterans' Night. Esme holds a dinner for us local vets twice a month."

"Esme is never late," Doug reported. "the Sutton Book Club is her life. She knows people rely on her."

The woman frowned. Ben was suddenly filled with dread.

"Did you attend her husband's funeral?" the man on the porch asked. "How did she seem?"

Doug and Ben now exchanged looks of panic.

"Larry died?" Ben asked.

The woman nodded. "I'm afraid so."

Doug made a strange noise in his throat. He'd encountered so much death over the years, but Ben understood that losing Larry felt personal. He'd been a necessary partner to Esme, who'd brought so much love to their lives.

"He was a good man," Ben said.

"How did he pass?" Doug asked.

"Heart attack," the man answered. "Two weeks ago."

"We were holed up at home for a while," Ben explained. "We didn't know." He was ashamed for not having helped Esme through this terrible time.

The woman took a tentative step down the porch stairs. For the first time, Ben saw something in her face— something familiar.

"My name is Rebecca Vance," she said. "My mother is Esme Gardner."

"Jesus," Doug muttered.

Rebecca eyed Doug with disbelief. "I don't suppose you're Doug Coleman?"

"You surprised I'm still alive?"

Rebecca laughed gently. Her father stepped up behind her and shoved his hands in his pockets. Doug's smile disappeared.

"I'm just glad to see you again. How are you holding up?" Rebecca asked.

"Still kicking," Doug reported.

Together, Rebecca, her father, Ben, and Doug observed the locked door of the Sutton House. Nobody wanted to admit just how concerned they were.

"I'm sure she's just at home," Rebecca said finally. She glanced back toward Doug and Ben. "Does she still live in the same place?"

"Since the day you left," Doug affirmed.

Rebecca's eyes watered. She turned toward her father, who nodded. "We'll head over there. Thanks for your help."

Ben and Doug turned and walked back to Doug's truck, leaving Rebecca and her father on the porch to mutter angrily and with confusion. Once in the truck, Doug grunted and glared up at them as though he didn't trust them as far as he could throw them. "Those Suttons were always so lost. They never knew how much love they had."

Ben cocked his head. "So that's Esme's first husband?"

"Poor excuse of a man if you ask me," Doug hissed. "Let's go back home, shall we? I have a can of beans with our name on it."

Ben burned with curiosity for these mystery Suttons. Even as he pulled out of the handicapped spot and drove back toward Doug's "estate," as he called it, Rebecca's question echoed in his mind. *Does she still live in the same place?* What kind of person didn't know where their mother lived? And what had happened in Esme's past to result in such broken relationships between mother and daughter?

Chapter Six

Rebecca and Victor had had a long day. They sat in the front seat of Rebecca's SUV in disbelief as an early evening sun dappled the front windshield. It was time to drive to the house they'd both spent significant years of their life in and face Esme.

"It's bizarre that she's not here," Rebecca muttered as she turned the keys. "She was always here when we were kids."

"Even stranger to see Doug still alive," Victor countered. "He must be a hundred years old. He looked at me like he hated me. Did you see that?"

Rebecca eyed Victor warily. Since their strained lunch at the diner that afternoon, she'd tried to keep conversation topics loose and easy. Now that they were on Nantucket, their emotions ran high.

The first sight of the Nantucket Sound sparkling on either side of the ferry had been nostalgic, yet painfully so. As the ferry motor roared, Victor and Rebecca had clung to the outside railing and watched the beautiful island come toward them, opening its arms in a way that made Rebecca ache. She'd suddenly longed to drop into the belly of the past and fix everything that had gone wrong even though it was probably too late.

"What year did Grandpa die?" Rebecca muttered as she drove. "It must have been fifteen, twenty years ago?"

"Thomas passed in 2006," Victor affirmed.

"I read about it. Fred and I talked about coming down for the funeral." Rebecca blinked away tears, remembering her grandfather and his iconic laugh.

"Why didn't you?"

"Honestly?" Rebecca glanced at her father. "I was terrified to face Mom and see Grandpa lying in a casket. I hadn't been back in years."

They drove in silence. Rebecca was astonished at the ease with which she took to the old streets. The route seemed to appear to her on instinct, guiding her to the beachside Victorian. In the driveway, Rebecca turned the engine off and peered at the dark-gray house with its sharply slanted rooftops and big bay windows that looked like eyes. As a child, she'd thought the house had a soul. She'd told her younger sisters it could talk. *What had she heard the house say?* She couldn't remember anymore. Her childhood magic had been lost a long time ago.

Rebecca and Victor walked to the front porch. Victor knocked on the porch railing, inspected the new paint job, and muttered, "Larry and Esme took pretty good care of the place over the years. I have to hand it to them."

"I'm sure they didn't do it for your sake," Rebecca said under her breath. *Why would they have?* Victor had abandoned this house. He had no say in how it had been taken care of.

"What was that? I couldn't hear you," Victor asked.

"Nothing." Rebecca pressed the doorbell and listened

as the sharp tune echoed through the halls. She craned her neck to hear the sound of footfalls or the creaking of the staircase, but it remained quiet.

"Huh." Victor shifted his weight and peered into the dark window.

"Don't do that. You don't want her to see you for the first time through the window," Rebecca pointed out.

"I don't think she's home," Victor said.

Rebecca pressed the doorbell again and again, but there was no sound of life within. "Maybe she went to the store," Rebecca tried. She pictured her mother loading a cart with cereal boxes and fresh fruit, greeting the woman at the cash register warmly and asking about every single member of the woman's family. "We can just wait in the car."

Instead of turning back to the SUV, Victor walked along the front porch and disappeared around the side. Each of his footfalls made the porch floorboards creak. Rebecca groaned. A frantic wind ripped through her hair, and she leafed for a hair tie in her pocket and tied her hair into a bun. The action reminded her so much of being a teenager, and she shivered with déjà vu. "Dad! Wait up."

Rebecca hurried around the side porch and found her father on the sand halfway between the Victorian and the rolling waves. Ordinarily, the Nantucket Sound was a peaceful expanse of silver and turquoise waters. But as evening fell and the winds escalated, waves had begun to roar to shore. Victor's gray hair flapped unceremoniously in the wind, and his suit jacket whipped open. Rebecca stepped down the porch steps one at a time and ran out toward him. Above, clouds huddled together, and it suddenly felt much later in the day.

"Dad?"

But she could see the water captivated him by how he gazed out across it with enormous eyes. Several thick rain-drops flashed across Rebecca's cheeks and forehead. "Dad, I think we should get under cover."

It was one of those frantic island storms. Growing up on Nantucket had meant understanding the ease with which a storm came and dissipated. It meant having sharp senses to notice a swift change.

"I forgot how beautiful it is," Victor breathed. He was barely loud enough against the scream of the wind and water.

Rebecca tugged on her father's elbow, and they raced back toward the Victorian home. The darkness intensified by the minute. Once they got to the porch, rain rattled across the rooftops and threatened to tear through the house. Victor's laughter echoed through the porch.

"This is quite a storm, Becca!" he cried. Nobody had called Rebecca that in forty years.

"I hope Mom's okay out in this," Rebecca called back.

"Your mother has Nantucket blood, same as I do," Victor said. "She'll be fine."

Rebecca remained very still, her hands at her sides as she watched the rain pound against her SUV. Around the Victorian were the same set of old colonials and Victorian styles with two- and three-story homes from Rebecca's youth, some updated with paint jobs and new bay windows. Perhaps the same families remained, too sure of the beauty of their surroundings to entertain a move else-where. Although Rebecca had given her heart to Bar Harbor, she couldn't blame them.

"Hey. Rebecca. Look at this!"

Rebecca turned to find her father bent, the doormat lifted to reveal a shining set of keys beneath.

"Dad. No." Rebecca shook her head as though she scolded a child.

"Come on, Becca. It's getting cold out here. Your mother wouldn't want us to get sick."

Rebecca crossed her arms over her chest and hissed. "I haven't been here since I was eighteen years old. You haven't been here in longer than that. We're basically strangers. It would be breaking in."

Victor already had the key in the lock. "I forgot how nice it felt to trust your neighbors."

"Dad!"

Victor stepped into the foyer and removed his shoes. Lightning slashed through the violent sky, and thunder made the house shake. Rebecca followed after her father and closed the door carefully behind her as though frightened it would break.

And just like that, she'd entered her own personal haunted house.

The old house had been built in the year 1867. For Rebecca, that had seemed like an impossible time period, so many years before her own grandfather had been born, and as a child, she'd been fascinated with imagining all the other children who'd ever lived in the old place. *What had their names been? What had they looked like?* Sometimes, she and her sisters pretended they lived in the Victorian in 1867, that their father was a whaler, and they eagerly awaited his homecoming after three years at sea. At the time, they hadn't known that one day, their father really would leave. They probably wouldn't have played the game if they had.

Victor eased through the shadows of the foyer, through the living room, and into the kitchen. Rebecca shrugged off her jacket and tiptoed through the house, noting Esme's beautiful design changes over the years. Over the fireplace hung a painting of sailboats at the Nantucket Regatta. Next to the baby grand piano hung a recent photograph of Larry and Esme, in which Esme wore a cream satin gown. She was, eternally, a knock-out.

"Dad?" Rebecca walked into the kitchen to find him filling two glasses with water.

Victor turned to pass one glass to Rebecca with red-rimmed eyes. "It's really something in here, isn't it? I can't believe she painted that burgundy accent wall. She begged me to do that for years, but I thought it would look tacky."

"It looks really good." Rebecca clutched her glass and eyed the burgundy living room wall, which you could see from the kitchen.

"I know. She was right. She was always right." Victor sipped his water.

Rebecca and Victor sat in the breakfast nook for the first hour or so and watched the storm from the back window. It was eerie in the big, creaking house, and Rebecca had demanded that her father not go exploring. "It's bad enough we came in."

After the storm cleared, Rebecca was certain Esme would return soon. She strained to hear the sound of the garage door opening or the rub of the tires over the driveway. She refilled her glass of water and checked the fridge, which was well-stocked with food. *Where in the world was her mother?*

When thirty minutes had passed, Victor stood and placed his glass of water on the counter with a clunk. He then returned to the living room.

"Where are you going?" Rebecca demanded. She was on edge, and her ears rang with panic.

"Just stretching my legs," he said.

But Rebecca knew better than to trust Victor Sutton. In a moment, she heard the creak of the first step on the staircase, followed by the *thunk-thunk-thunk* of his body moving to the second floor. Rebecca groaned and rushed after him, readying her demands that he return downstairs. But when she got to the second floor, she found him standing in the doorway of what had once been her bedroom, and something very hard and cold within her melted.

In that old house, Victor was a slave to his memories, just as Rebecca was.

"Look." Victor opened the door wider to reveal the bedroom. Rebecca stepped forward to peer around her father at a room that seemed only partially in the twenty-first century. On the far wall hung a bulletin board where Rebecca had pinned forty or fifty photographs of herself, her friends, and her sisters. It showed them at prom, some on horseback, then at the beach with their adolescent bodies tanned and toned to perfection. Rebecca couldn't breathe. She entered the stale air of the room and stared at the photographs, muttering, "Why didn't she take these down?"

But Rebecca knew the answer. Removing the photographs meant Rebecca's time in Nantucket was over. Removing the photographs acknowledged what no mother wanted to—that her baby was grown-up and gone.

Shame spiraled in Rebecca's stomach. She dropped onto the edge of the bed and looked around at the other trinkets left in her bedroom—several cookbooks she'd dog-eared and scribbled in, a yearbook from 1994, and a Nantucketers baseball hat she'd stolen from an old boyfriend. When Lily had dated in high school, Rebecca had scolded her to give old boyfriends' sweatshirts and hats back. She hadn't realized how hypocritical she was.

Victor had left her bedroom. Rebecca heaved a sigh and patted the old bedspread, then headed to the doorway, assuming Victor had just gone to Bethany's or Valerie's bedroom. But when she stepped into the hallway, she found Victor at the far end. His head was in the crack of the doorway, but he kept his feet at a distance as though frightened the room would eat him alive.

Rebecca shook violently. She'd been annoyed at her father's curiosity and his digging around. But she hadn't expected him to be so violent in his meddling. She hadn't expected him to open that door.

Rebecca hustled down the hallway. She felt wordless, enraged. Just before she reached Victor, she got a single glance into the room, one that revealed it to be every bit the same as it always had been—through the eighties and into the nineties. It was akin to a museum with no item out of place. Victor turned to reveal panicked eyes. Before he could speak, Rebecca grabbed the knob and slammed the door back in place. The sound ricocheted up and down the hallway.

Chapter Seven

It was now eleven at night. Another storm churned across the island, and the house shivered around them. Rebecca and Victor sat sullenly. They'd hardly spoken since the incident upstairs.

"We should go get a hotel room," Rebecca suggested, although exhaustion from the day kept her glued to the chair.

Victor was quiet. He stood from the breakfast table and headed for the cabinet, an antique passed down from Grandpa Thomas's mother. Rebecca's stomach gurgled and groaned.

"We can't take her stuff," Rebecca said, her tone firm. But already, Victor opened the cabinet and removed a beautiful bottle of red wine, a sleeve of crackers, and a jar of olives. He set the items across the counter and opened the fridge, which Rebecca again noted was so well-stocked that it was unlikely Esme had to go to the store. He removed a brie and some gouda and, with practiced ease, began to assemble a cheese platter.

"Your mother and I ate like this frequently after we had you," he explained as he plopped olives into a small ornate bowl. "We didn't have the energy to cook. Isn't it funny that, after those origins, you turned into such a marvelous chef?"

"Mom is a great cook," Rebecca countered.

"She is quite good," Victor admitted. "But she would be floored with your work. It's a real pity she was never able to see Bar Harbor Brasserie before you closed it."

Rebecca blinked back tears. She'd hardly realized how much she'd wanted her mother to enter Bar Harbor Brasserie's front doors, hug Fred and her babies, and enjoy a meal. She hadn't realized how much she'd wanted to serve her now that she couldn't.

Victor uncorked the wine bottle at the table and poured them stiff glasses. Rebecca accepted the glass and allowed herself to look her father in the eye. She knew exactly what he was thinking about because she was thinking about it, too. The room upstairs. *How was it possible it looked exactly the same? How was it possible so much time had passed?*

"To ghosts," Victor said as he raised his glass.

Rebecca didn't say anything. She sipped, coating her tongue with an Italian grape that would have impressed Fred. Victor chewed an olive and smeared brie across a thick cracker heavy with seeds. As they drank and ate, they didn't speak. Rebecca abandoned her worries about breaking and entering into her mother's house and instead decided to worry about her mother's whereabouts. *Where could a woman of Esme's age be at such a late hour?*

"We can't be too worried," Victor tried, reading Rebecca's mind. "We didn't tell her we were coming, and we haven't been in contact for years. She didn't exactly clear her schedule."

Rebecca nodded and placed a slab of cheese on her tongue. Slowly, the sustenance made her think more clearly. Her phone buzzed with a text from Shelby, who sent a photograph of a roaring campfire in the Acadia Mountains, along with a write-up of how her first two days had gone. Her happiness calmed Rebecca. Without prompting, she turned the phone around to show the photograph to Victor, who smiled.

"You've got an outdoorsy girl," he commented.

"She takes after her father." Rebecca darkened her phone and looked out the window at a wild-limbed oak that swayed back and forth in the wind. Lily, Shelby, and Chad would have loved this place. They would have loved their grandmother. *Why had she drawn such a harsh boundary between her new family and her past?*

The cheese plate cleared, and their first glasses of wine were now empty as Victor stood and again receded into the darkness. Rebecca sat in the silence of herself for a little while and refilled her glass of wine. When Victor had been gone for ten minutes, she stood and traced his path, no longer angry with him for roaming the halls. What they'd done in the past was considerably worse than this. And worry for her mother's safety overshadowed every other emotion.

She found Victor in the same place she'd always found him as a girl. He sat at the antique mahogany desk in the study, tilted gently forward to lean on one elbow and peer out the window. Just as ever, volumes of books lined the shelves, the ones too ornate and valuable to keep at the Sutton Book Club. The air was stiff with dust.

"How many hours did you spend in here?" Rebecca surprised herself with the soft question.

Victor laughed sadly. "Thousands? Millions?"

Rebecca stepped forward and scanned the book titles. She found Shakespearean, Beckett, and Brecht plays and novels from Hemingway and Fitzgerald. There was a signed copy of *The Lord of the Rings*, a text her grandfather had adored due to its parallels to the horrors of World War II.

"I started my career here," Victor said wistfully. "I was so hungry to make my life into something spectacular. Your mother always said she didn't set out to marry someone with such ambition."

"Oh, but she loved your ambition," Rebecca remembered.

Victor grimaced. The shadows of the dark room made his wrinkles far more prominent. "I missed so many hours with my young family while in this room."

Rebecca's breathing was irregular. She steadied herself against the bookshelf nearest the desk and tried to think of something to say to her father. Something that wasn't a sarcastic, *Guess you shouldn't have run off with your personal assistant, huh? Poor guy.*

Instead, Rebecca managed, "Yes, in this room, you also built your family psychologist empire."

Victor scoffed gently. "Your grandfather was very well-connected in fields of academia. A friend of his wrote a review of my very first book as a favor to him."

Rebecca didn't know this story.

"Nobody suspected the book would take off the way it did," Victor continued. "Nobody except your mother."

"She always said you were a brilliant writer."

"I'm sure she didn't say that after I left," Victor said quietly.

"She did. Whenever Bethany, Valerie, or I wrote a paper for school, she complimented our writing styles. It was always, *'You got this from your father.'*"

Victor lifted his eyes to Rebecca's. He looked wounded and regretful, as though he no longer wanted to be there.

"This isn't going the way you thought it would, is it?" Rebecca asked timidly.

Victor ruffled his hair. "Nothing ever does."

Rebecca scanned the mahogany desk, which held no history of Victor's time. A photograph of Grandpa Thomas in his war uniform sat in the corner alongside a picture of a dog Rebecca didn't recognize. She'd been gone so long that Esme could have raised two puppies to old age without Rebecca being any wiser. A calendar of events on the upper-righthand corner listed dentist appointments for both Esme and Larry.

"What's this?" Rebecca bent to read a piece of paper removed from an envelope. It was official-looking, addressed from the State of Massachusetts to Esme and Larry Gardner.

Rebecca knew better than to read her mother's mail. But the words: **NOTICE OF EVICTION** forced her eyes. According to the state, the current tenants of the old colonial building that housed the Sutton Book Club were behind on taxes, rent, and other miscellaneous fees. If the calculations were correct, Esme owed one hundred and eleven thousand dollars plus change.

Rebecca's jaw dropped. "Dad? Are you seeing this?"

Victor read the letter and tugged on his beard. "It doesn't make any sense."

"Why not?"

"Nantucket always upheld the historical importance of the Sutton Book Club. Your grandfather had a wonderful relationship with the Nantucket Historical Society, who ensured donations were available for the Sutton Book Club and its many neighborhood programs."

Rebecca shook her head. "So the Sutton Book Club never made its own income?"

"Your grandfather never wanted to ask for money from Nantucketers. He saw the Sutton Book Club as part library and part community center. It was a meeting place. A world of literature and ideas that brought people together. I imagine your mother has kept the same model."

"But you would think she would eventually find a way to make money with it," Rebecca reasoned. "I mean, once you're fifty thousand in the red, wouldn't you make a change?"

Victor shrugged. "Your mother was always an idealist. Maybe she thought an investor would swoop in and save the day."

"Why do you think the Nantucket Historical Society stopped supporting the Sutton Book Club?" Rebecca asked.

"I hate to say it follows a pattern, doesn't it? The rest of the world cares very little for literature these days. I imagine someone else took over the historical society and implanted their own set of rules. Maybe that money went to a new boardwalk or a new ferry boat. Something to keep the tourists happy, rather than the locals."

Rebecca's heart fluttered. "It seems so cruel."

"To us, maybe," Victor agreed. "But we're the Suttons.

We think the world revolves around your grandfather's set of books in that beautiful colonial house."

"Even after so many years away, I was pretty sure everything about the Sutton Book Club would be the same," Rebecca admitted.

Chapter Eight

Given the lateness of the hour and the ongoing storm, it was ridiculous to do anything but stay the night. Rebecca stretched clean sheets over the guest room bed and shoved pillows into pillowcases, her mind heavy with the news from the letter. *Had her mother run away from her problems? Had she gone somewhere to fix it?*

Victor wore a pair of pajama pants and a loose T-shirt. His face washed and his teeth scrubbed, he looked sweet and soft and docile, not like the man she'd demonized all these years. Rebecca waved to him as he walked toward the guest room. "The bed is ready for you."

"Thank you." Victor's cheek twitched. For a moment, Rebecca panicked he would say he loved her, something he'd done so easily for the first years of her life.

"Sleep well." Rebecca hustled past him and rushed upstairs. She entered her childhood bedroom and sat on the bed for a long time, focusing on her breath. When her phone read 12:30 a.m., she undressed and donned one of Fred's large T-shirts and a pair of shorts, then slipped under the covers. The clean and crisp sheets weren't a surprise. Esme had always been a wonderful homemaker, the sort who dusted even the corners guests didn't see. Rebecca had tried and failed to be that sort of mother and wife over the years. Fred had picked up the slack, bless him.

Rebecca slept fitfully. Every gust of wind against the house and every violent creak from a tree limb outside rattled her. Around three thirty, car lights outside convinced her that her mother was finally home, and she stood at the top of the staircase, listening and waiting. When nobody came inside, Rebecca cursed her anxious imagination and returned to bed.

For Rebecca, restless sleep was common. As a chef, anxiety and stress often skyrocketed during busy evenings at Bar Harbor Brasserie and made it difficult for her to calm when she hit the sack. Having teenage children didn't help. Add Fred's death, Victor's spontaneous return, and Esme's disappearance, and you didn't have a recipe for an easy sleep. This was nightmare territory.

Rebecca awoke with a start at seven thirty. The storm had passed, and the glittering June sunlight cut through her bedroom curtains. A poster of a *Titanic*-era Leonardo Dicaprio hanging on her closet door welcomed her to a brand-new day. The ink on the old poster had faded after thirty years and now looked vintage.

Rebecca padded downstairs and checked the garage. Still no Esme. In the kitchen, the coffee pot bubbled, and her father sat with the newspaper splayed in front of him on the kitchen table. The year in that kitchen could have been 1995, except that the paper had been addressed to LARRY GARDNER instead of VICTOR SUTTON.

"What's the news, Dad?"

"Nantucket High is building a new athletic center," Victor said. "I wonder if that's where the money from the Sutton Book Club is going?"

Rebecca took two mugs from the cabinet. One featured the Leaning Tower of Pisa, and the other was covered in music notes. *When had Esme gone to Pisa?*

"I think we should go next door." Rebecca watched the last droplets of coffee drip into the pot. "Maybe she told the neighbors where she was off to."

Victor grunted. It occurred to Rebecca that Victor had nowhere else to go—that he was hiding out in the wake of his divorce in the last "home" he'd known. He'd decided to try on his old life like an old glove. *Did it fit him? Did it fit either of them?* Rebecca didn't know.

Rebecca sipped her coffee and texted her kids. Lily had begun her internship and loved being back in the city. Shelby had found a tick on her hairline that morning but had removed it promptly. Chad, who texted the least of all her children, sent a selfie of him on a basketball court with his tongue out. Rebecca smiled and wrote back, "My one-of-a-kind son."

After they dressed, Rebecca and Victor met in the foyer to approach one of the neighbors. Victor seemed hesitant, like an anxious dog. "Why don't we try the Petersons?" Victor pointed at the house to the left.

But when they knocked on the Petersons's door, nobody came. A sign on the mailbox said "the Gregors," anyway, which wasn't a family Rebecca or Victor had ever heard of.

"Let's talk to Mr. and Mrs. Walton," Rebecca suggested, pointing at the brick house to the right of theirs.

Victor groaned.

"What?" Rebecca demanded. "They were always over for dinner."

"Mark Walton was about as dull as they come," Victor said.

Rebecca rolled her eyes and shot out through the lawn. It was wet from the storm and the morning dew, and it dampened the bottom of her jeans. "It looks like someone mowed recently," she said. Victor was quiet.

Rebecca was relieved when she saw the sign that read "The Waltons" still hanging on the front door. She rang the doorbell, and immediately, a dog yapped wildly in the back.

"They always had the most annoying dogs," Victor muttered.

A moment later, a woman in her seventies opened the door and peered through the crack. Her yappy dog bounced behind her legs. "Hello?"

"Hi! Mrs. Walton? You probably don't remember me. My name is Rebecca Sutton." Rebecca stuttered over her last name.

Mrs. Walton's eyes widened. The dog's yapping reached another decibel. "Rebecca! My goodness." She opened the door a little bit wider. "Where on earth have you been?"

Rebecca laughed gently as Mrs. Walton's eyes shifted toward Victor. Immediately, her face tightened with anger. "Victor Sutton, as I live and breathe. I'd recognize you anywhere."

"Hello, Beatrice." Victor crossed his arms over his chest. "You're looking well."

The air between them was thick with tension.

"Have you come back to pester that wonderful woman?" Mrs. Walton asked icily.

"We don't want to pester her. We're worried about her," Rebecca tried.

"Worried? Esme Gardner has always done well for herself," Mrs. Walton pointed out.

"We recently learned about her husband's death," Rebecca continued timidly.

Mrs. Walton's eyes were pained. "Larry was a remarkable man and oh, so healthy. He was always out running along the beach or tending to his garden. Goes to show you that life has its way with all of us." She cleared her throat. "I went to the funeral a couple of weeks back."

"How did Mom seem?" Rebecca asked.

"Strong as an ox," Mrs. Walton reported. "She had some friends over for dinner after the burial. We stayed up all hours of the night, talking about the good old times." She again glared at Victor as though she wanted him to know just how many good times Esme had had after he'd left.

Rebecca bit her lower lip. "Thank you for supporting my mother during that horrible time."

Mrs. Walton sniffed.

"We really do need to find her," Rebecca continued. "We arrived yesterday and assumed we would catch her at the Sutton Book Club."

"She's normally there. So committed to the Book Club, just like her father was," Mrs. Walton said.

"But it was closed," Rebecca countered. "And she never came home last night. Did she tell you about a trip she had planned? I know Nantucket neighbors always watch out for each other."

Mrs. Walton frowned. "She didn't mention anything."

Silence fell between the three of them. Rebecca's heartbeat escalated.

"But I just saw her yesterday morning," Mrs. Walton continued. "She got her mail around one in the afternoon like she always does, and we waved like we always do."

"Did she seem like her normal self?" Rebecca asked.

"How would you know what her normal self is like?" Mrs. Walton demanded.

Rebecca's cheeks burned with shame. Mrs. Walton's comment was completely warranted.

"Listen. Do you have her cell phone number, at least?" Rebecca asked.

Mrs. Walton disappeared into the shadows of the house. The tiny terrier approached and sniffed Rebecca's ankles as Victor grumbled about how much he'd always disliked Beatrice. They didn't have to ask where Beatrice's husband was; it was apparent he was no longer around.

Mrs. Walton returned to the front door with her cell phone. Esme's phone number sat on the screen in big block numbers. Rebecca took a photograph of it with her cell and thanked the woman profusely.

"Losing Larry has been hard on all of us," Mrs. Walton finished as she pocketed her phone. "He was a marvelous and caring neighbor. He always went out of his way for you. Always smiled." Again, she glared at Victor, who made sure not to smile back.

"We'll just be next door if you hear anything," Rebecca told Mrs. Walton. "Don't hesitate to come over if you need..." She trailed off as the dog yapped violently.

Rebecca and Victor returned home. Once inside, Victor watched as Rebecca called Esme's phone number and pressed the phone to her ear. There had to be an explanation for all of this. After all, Mrs. Walton had just seen Esme less than twenty-four hours ago.

Immediately, the call went to voicemail. Rebecca's stomach clenched. She tried the number again, but again had no answer. Esme's cheerful (if slightly older) voice asked the caller to leave their name and number. She would get back to them soon. Rebecca hung up.

"Something's wrong," Rebecca insisted.

Victor sighed and palmed his neck.

"I mean, how do we know we're not in the middle of a serious emergency?" Rebecca demanded.

"We don't," Victor admitted.

"I'm calling the police."

"She could have left the island to visit someone," Victor suggested.

"She would have told her neighbor," Rebecca said.

"I don't know if your mother liked Mrs. Walton any more than I did."

Rebecca's nostrils flared. She turned away from him, already with her phone to her ear. *What did her father know about Esme's new life? What did Rebecca know?* She felt as though she was free-falling through another dimension. The responsible thing was to call.

Within the hour, two police officers appeared on the porch. Rebecca opened the door to greet them, then shrieked with surprise when she realized they were familiar.

"Franklin? Conner?" Rebecca opened the door wider and regarded the middle-aged men, who she'd seen red-faced and out-of-their-minds drunk at beach parties in summers long past. They were now middle-aged, just as she was. Conner had lost quite a bit of his hair.

"Rebecca?" Franklin gaped in disbelief.

"I never thought I'd see the day." Conner gave Rebecca a half smile.

"They let you two become police officers?" Rebecca beckoned for them to enter.

"We joined the force together," Franklin explained.

"At twenty-four," Conner offered. He placed his hands on his sides and surveyed the living room. Victor sat on the piano bench and nodded dully. Conner's smile dropped.

Franklin eyed Rebecca's hand. "I see you're married. We both are, too."

"And too many kids between us," Conner noted with a laugh. "They just kept coming."

Rebecca saw no reason to tell these ghosts from her past about Fred. Instead, she laughed and congratulated them, then slowly shifted to the topic at-hand.

"We came to visit Mom, but she never came home last night. We're worried."

Franklin and Conner exchanged glances. "Are you suggesting she's a missing person?" Conner asked.

Rebecca stuttered with disbelief. "I don't know. Her neighbor saw her yesterday, but—"

As Rebecca stuttered, Franklin's and Conner's expressions grew harder, less welcoming.

"When was the last time you saw your mother, Rebecca?" Conner inquired.

"Oh. Gosh. It's been longer than I'd like to admit." Rebecca swallowed.

"Esme Gardner is an esteemed member of this community. As guardians of that community, we must respect her privacy," Franklin continued.

"And I imagine she wouldn't be too keen on her ex-husband and her estranged daughter meddling in her business," Conner finished.

Rebecca's mouth was very dry. "I just can't imagine where she would have gone. Her phone keeps going to voicemail."

Conner waved his hands. "We at the Nantucket Police Force know better than to get involved with Sutton family drama."

Franklin chortled. "You know it."

Conner turned on his heel and headed for the door. Franklin followed him, his keys jangling from his belt.

"What if she doesn't come back tonight?" Rebecca demanded. "Or tomorrow?"

Franklin turned back to lock eyes with her. "Listen, Rebecca. Everyone on this island knows all about the Suttons. Everyone knows that Esme has lived a much better and happier life without you. If you don't hear from Esme right now, I have to assume that's by choice. Esme doesn't want to be found."

Rebecca's voice cracked. "But we're worried about her!"

Franklin and Conner exchanged glances. "Nothing bad ever happens in Nantucket, Rebecca. You know that."

"But we'll reach out to her ourselves," Conner affirmed. "If we find it necessary."

Stunned, Rebecca made her way to the front door and watched as they ambled to their cop car. They seemed self-satisfied, as though they'd stood up for a member of their community in a way that upheld their state and their constitution. Rebecca bit her lip and felt another wave of worry fall over her. Nobody, it seemed, could help her find Esme.

Behind her, Victor put on his shoes. "I'm going for a walk," he announced. "I have to get out of this godforsaken house."

Rebecca stepped back and watched him. He raked his fingers through his gray hair as he walked out the front door, his face stoic. For a moment, as he grew smaller on the walkway and disappeared down the sidewalk, Rebecca was grateful he was gone. He was the source of her family's poison. *As their father, wasn't he supposed to be the one who put them back together again?* But in a moment, as the immense house and its cataclysmic memories shrouded her, she shivered with loneliness. At the piano bench, she studied the beautiful photograph of her mother and Larry, her mother's eyes alight with promise for a day she could never get back.

Where on earth was she? And why was it suddenly so necessary that Rebecca find her and repair the damage they'd wrought?

Chapter Nine

Five years ago, in a moment of weakness, Rebecca had added her two little sisters as friends on Facebook. Both Bethany and Valerie had agreed to Rebecca's friend requests, but neither had written a thing. Such was the way of the Sutton family.

At the time, Lily had been sixteen and a terror. She'd gotten into two car accidents in the span of two months and was obsessed with the fact that nobody understood her. Rebecca even caught her smoking pot. "It reminds me of being a teenager," Rebecca had sighed to Fred. "Gosh, my sisters and I used to get in so much trouble."

Rebecca, Bethany, and Valerie Sutton were Nantucket's Sutton sisters. At one time, they were well-known in every establishment around the island, which allowed them free ice cream cones, funny banter with shop clerks, french fries served on the house, and free rides home from friends of their father and mother. They were tanned and beautiful, each with singular talents and very long, wavy brunette hair. Although they each had unique facial features, they could have been nothing but sisters. They came as a unit. To everyone, it seemed they would take on the world.

Of the three, Bethany was probably the most academic and responsible. At summer beach parties, it had always been Bethany who reeled Rebecca in, demanding they head home before Esme came to check on them. Fittingly, Bethany had gone to medical school and become a surgeon in Savannah, Georgia. She'd married a surgeon and had three genius children.

Now, Rebecca pulled up Bethany's Facebook. A profile picture displayed a beautiful and wholesome-looking woman next to a similarly handsome and wholesome-looking man. They spent their days saving people's lives on the operating table. *Would Bethany even find space in her heart to care about what was happening on Nantucket? Had she fully turned her back on the Suttons?*

Bethany's profile listed her phone number. Rebecca typed it with shaking fingers and listened as it rang and rang across the East Coast. When Bethany didn't answer, Rebecca collapsed on the living room couch and reassessed. *Why would Bethany answer a phone call from a number she didn't recognize?*

REBECCA: Hi, Bethany. It's your sister Rebecca. Could you give me a call?

Within a minute, Bethany called back. "Rebecca?" She sounded like she was in a crowded place. Voices buzzed and echoed around the phone.

"Bethany. Thank goodness you called." Tears filled Rebecca's eyes. Bethany's voice had ripped her through time.

"Are you okay?" Bethany was slightly breathless, as though she walked very quickly.

"I don't know. I don't." Rebecca wished she'd

rehearsed how to tell her sister any of this. Instead, she heard herself blurt, "My husband died."

"Oh." Bethany's tone dropped. Suddenly, the voices around her were gone, and there was only silence. "Oh, Rebecca. I'm so sorry. Really." She paused again. "I know I never knew him. But I saw all the photos of you guys on Facebook, and I always thought you looked so happy."

Rebecca's heart seized. She wasn't sure if what Bethany said made anything better or worse. "Yeah. It's been rough."

"Are you still in Bar Harbor? What's going on? Do you, um... Do you need me to come visit?" She asked it so readily.

Rebecca stuttered. "Kind of. Sort of. But I'm not in Bar Harbor right now." She cleared her throat, then asked, "Are you ready for a doozy of a story?"

Bethany moaned. "I guess I have to be."

Over the next five minutes, Rebecca explained the current situation. She spoke of the debilitating months since Fred's death, of closing the restaurant, and of Victor's spontaneous arrival. She acknowledged Victor had probably only "picked" Rebecca because she was in a weaker state, but she added she had little else to do and nowhere else to be. Besides, Esme's husband had died, and it seemed as good a time as any to see Esme again and attempt to salvage their relationship.

"I think that's fair," Bethany tried.

"But Mom's missing." Rebecca's voice broke. "Dad and I got here yesterday. She hasn't been home even though she has a stocked fridge, and the neighbor just saw her. The cops don't want to get involved in our family's business, and Dad seems increasingly sullen. Oh, did I mention he's getting divorced?"

"What!" It was Bethany's turn to sound panicked. "But I thought Bree was the love of his life or whatever?"

Rebecca snorted grateful her sister understood how sour she felt about Bree. "I hate to ask you to come with all the ghosts this place has. But I really, really need you here."

Bethany was quiet for a while. Rebecca could feel her teetering between yes and no. How dare her eldest sister interrupt her perfect life and demand attention?

Then again, Bethany was a healer. She was a helper. She couldn't not come. *Right?*

"I wish you would have called me when Fred died," Bethany said instead.

"I should have. I was drowning."

"And now you're on Nantucket."

"Even deeper underwater," Rebecca agreed. "Look at the mess I've made."

Bethany sighed. "All right. Tell you what. I have two surgeries this afternoon. Everything else this week can be set to the side."

Rebecca's jaw dropped. "So... you can come?"

"I'll grab a flight first thing tomorrow."

Rebecca closed her eyes, overwhelmed by this act of generosity.

"Have you called Val?" Bethany asked.

"Do you think she'll even care?"

Bethany groaned. "I don't even know where she lives right now. Is she still in Las Vegas?"

"Her Facebook profile says Seattle," Rebecca said. "But who knows?"

"Good luck," Bethany said with a sigh. "I have to call my husband and explain what's up. But I'll send you my ferry details tomorrow. Meet me at the docks?"

"I'll meet you at the docks," Rebecca affirmed.

* * *

True to form, Valerie didn't answer her phone. Rebecca gave up after the seventh ring and studied her littlest sister's profile picture, which featured her on a beach in a bikini and a pair of Audrey Hepburn sunglasses. As a teenager, a modeling agent had told Valerie she had the "it" factor and asked to take her on as a client. When it had come time for their first meeting, Valerie had gone to a beach party instead. "I don't want to feel like someone owns me," she'd said.

Of all the Sutton sisters, Valerie was the wildest of them. According to her Facebook, she'd spent her twenties and thirties bouncing from city to city, job to job, and relationship to relationship. Articles in established magazines such as *Wedding Today*, *The Wall Street Journal*, *The Guardian*, and many others called her one of the most exciting event planners of her generation. The party she'd planned after Coachella in 2009 was still discussed as one to beat. She'd been hired to plan Madonna's niece's wedding and Adele's best friend's. Still, from what Rebecca could glean, Valerie spent as much time out of work as she spent with it—which couldn't have been healthy for her crazy lifestyle.

Rebecca had confessed to Fred many times over the years how she worried about Valerie. *Why hadn't she reached out?* A Facebook friend request now seemed pathetic.

Rebecca took a break from calling on old ghosts and made herself an omelet. From the kitchen window, she watched a flock of seagulls bounce around the golden

Nantucket sands. Tourists in flashing windbreakers marched in little groups, and in the distance, sailboats darted beneath the blue sky.

Rebecca sliced extra vegetables and grated more cheese to make Victor an omelet. *How long had he been gone? Two hours? Three?* Rebecca walked to the foyer and peered out onto the driveway, where her SUV remained parked. Mrs. Walton walked slowly to her mailbox as her terrier nipped at her heels. "Don't do this to me, Dad," Rebecca breathed. She then stepped out onto the porch and waved at Mrs. Walton. "How is your day going?"

Mrs. Walton staggered toward the dividing line between their properties. "I saw you had the police over."

Rebecca nodded. "We're worried about Mom."

Mrs. Walton's eyes flashed. This was real gossip, the kind she could spend all afternoon calling people about. "Strange to see that father of yours around here. He looks like a dog with his tail between his legs."

Rebecca asked that Mrs. Walton let her know if she heard anything from her mother. She then returned to the kitchen to store the extra omelet ingredients in the fridge, promising herself Victor was just around the corner.

But Rebecca didn't hear from Victor until seven thirty that night. She'd been breathless when she answered her phone with an outraged, "Dad? Where the heck have you been?"

"Hello." The voice on the other line was not Victor's. "I'm calling from the Sunset Cove Bar. I take it this man is your father?"

Rebecca's heart dropped into her stomach. "You've got to be kidding me," she muttered.

"What?"

"Nothing." She swallowed. "Is he okay?"

"He's fine. He's just got the drunken blues, is all. I can't have him bumming out all the tourists," the man continued.

"I'll be right there."

Rebecca drove in silence. All afternoon, she'd walked around the main floor of that big house, her eyes glancing out the windows, terrified. Yes, the past dictated she wasn't Victor Sutton's biggest fan, but she didn't want anything to happen to him. She didn't want to add another layer to the tragedies of her year.

The Sunset Cove Bar bustled with sunburnt tourists and laughing honeymooners. Televisions hanging above the bar top counters displayed professional sports and flashy commercials. Rebecca felt like a fish out of water. Many years ago, she and Bethany had snuck into the bar with fake IDs, only to have a friend of their mother's recognize them at the counter and send them back home.

"Dad?" Victor Sutton looked defeated. He slumped on the counter with his fist against his cheek and his eyes glazed. A half-drunk beer sat in front of him, as did an unpaid bill. Rebecca inspected it, impressed with how much her father had knocked back before the bartender had asked to call someone.

Rebecca said it again. "Dad?"

And this time, Victor jumped and turned to meet her gaze. He smiled softly, drunkenly, as though he'd missed her. "Becca!" He then turned quickly to address the bartender. "This is my darling daughter. She's a chef, you know. A brilliant one, at that."

The bartender dully regarded Rebecca, then pointed at the bill on the counter. "Can you make sure to pay that before you go?"

Assisting her dad reminded Rebecca of picking up

her children at daycare. Slowly, she coaxed Victor into his coat, helped him find his wallet, and thanked the bartender twice for his help. As they ambled through the crowd, Victor squeezed her upper arm and rasped, "I'm so sorry, Rebecca. I'm so sorry." His smile crumpled.

"Dad. It's okay." She wanted it desperately to be okay even though it wasn't.

When they reached the SUV, Victor stumbled onto the passenger seat and pressed his hands over his heart. He gasped for breath. "I just can't believe it. I just can't believe it." He said this over and over again as his eyes searched the darkening horizon.

Rebecca wasn't sure exactly what he meant, but she got the point. So much time had passed, and so much had happened. Their family had been destroyed—and even Rebecca's and Victor's attempts to build families elsewhere had been thwarted. She started the engine as exhaustion enveloped her. And as she eased down a street she'd once known so well, she whispered, "It's going to be okay, Dad. I promise you." She said it, although she knew it wasn't true.

Chapter Ten

Summer rainstorms had their way with Doug's old house. They shattered windows, flung the shutters to the sand, and made roof tiles drop like leaves. Since Ben had moved in several years ago, he'd struggled against the weather, mending floorboards and patching shingles. But every newfound disaster whittled him down a bit more.

That morning, Ben woke up, shuffled downstairs, and discovered Doug's bed wet with rainwater from a ceiling leak. Doug stared at the mess, disgusted yet too fragile to move. He gestured at the hole in the ceiling as though expected.

"Won't be long till the sea eats this house whole," he said.

Ben hustled for Doug's wheelchair, which he propped up beside Doug's bed. He then helped Doug out of the damp bed, ripped off the sheets, raised the mattress from the bed frame, and wheeled Doug to the bathroom to change and clean himself up. Although Doug usually preferred to walk around by himself, something about the morning made him especially stiff. Now in his forties, Ben had begun to understand that.

"Why didn't you ring the bell when you woke up?" Ben demanded of Doug. "I would have immediately come to help."

"I was in the war," Doug shot back. "I can handle a bit of rain."

Ben grumbled. In the kitchen, he made Doug a bowl of porridge with fresh fruits and peanut butter and brewed a pot of coffee. Out the window, a blue-sky morning played in contrast to the sorry state of the old house.

After Ben set Doug up on the front porch with break-fast and the daily newspaper, Ben called the repairman Andy, whose family business had been in charge of Nantucket residences for fifty-five years. Unfortunately, Andy had had to change his prices with the economy, and Ben and Doug were not always able to keep up. This had brewed resentment and ill will between Ben and Andy, who'd previously been friendly.

"I hope you have good news for me, Ben," Andy said.

Ben grimaced. *When did he ever have good news?* "Doug's bedroom ceiling has a hole. He woke up with a soaking-wet mattress."

Andy coughed into the phone. "That's not what I wanted to hear."

"Do you have time to look at it?"

"The better question is will you ever pay me back for the past six months of repairs?"

Ben grimaced. It was true the old house had needed a multitude of expensive repairs over the winter. Their heater had cut out, a few pipes had burst, and a tree had blasted through the back window.

"And last I checked, that house is on its way to condemn town," Andy continued. "That ceiling is probably the tip of the iceberg."

Silence fell. In the background, some of Andy's family members barked orders at each other in the repair shop.

"I can try to fix it myself," Ben said.

Andy's tone softened. "Listen, man. I'm sorry. But things are tight for everyone right now. I can't just repair everything in that old house without going bankrupt."

"Yeah, man. Thanks." Ben hung up without waiting for a reply. Out on the front porch, Doug whistled sweetly to himself and flipped the newspaper. Ben's love for the old man was familiar. He felt like Andy and his repairman family had gone out of their way to attack him.

Rage toward Andy and exhaustion fought for first place on Ben's emotional roster. He stomped to Doug's bedroom and peered at the hole, which seemed larger now than ten minutes ago. He decided to set the bed frame up in the living room. As soon as the mattress dried out, he would return it to its frame.

He and Doug would make do, just as they always had before. Doug was right. They'd gone to war, so they could handle anything.

Ben stepped out onto the porch. The sun glittered across the Nantucket Sound and demanded attention. They couldn't possibly spend the day shifting and creaking through the old, nearly condemned house. They had to get out there and pretend they would live forever.

A few hours later, Ben parked Doug's truck near the pier. Despite Doug's pride, his exhaustion from lack of sleep had made him agree to be in a wheelchair so Ben could walk a longer distance. "I know it helps your image with the ladies if they see you wheeling an old man around," Doug suggested as Ben helped him into the chair.

"If you think for a second any ladies have their eye on me, you're delusional," Ben said. "They're all after you."

"They're after me for my money," Doug joked as he adjusted himself in the wheelchair. "Bunch of gold diggers."

"I'm sure they'll love the skylight you put in your bedroom," Ben said.

Doug gasped with laughter and wagged his eyebrows.

After locking the truck, Ben wheeled Doug along the boardwalk and paused at the little ice cream stand. It was a deliriously beautiful day, unseasonably warm, and he and Doug sat with their soft serves and watched the tourists as they showed off their pretty outfits and boat shoes, eyeing one another.

"It's like watching Animal Planet," Doug joked.

"Don't make fun of them too much. Most of them have so much money that they rule the world," Ben said.

"All the more reason to make fun of them," Doug pointed out. "They're so sure that money will keep them happy forever. I wish them good luck with that."

After their ice cream, Ben wheeled Doug toward the lighthouse, where they stood wordlessly against the railing and watched the water propel itself against the jagged rocks. Ben thought about his years in Afghanistan, and how he'd ached to see a body of water and to feel rain upon his face. By contrast, Doug had served in Europe, where water and wind had been prime players in the war that had changed the world forever. Once, Ben had asked

Doug if he felt he was a part of history. Doug had said, "That's a creative way of calling me old, isn't it?"

A part of Ben wanted to ask Doug what he thought they should do about the house. But another didn't want to ruin the beauty of this moment. There they stood—two men, aged forty-six and ninety-eight, enjoying a time of peace. The drama would come for them when it needed to.

On the way back to the truck, Doug pointed at a woman who walked erratically. Her hair shot out wildly in many directions as though she'd walked headlong into the wind, and her eyes were alert, animated.

"Isn't that Esme's daughter?"

It was. The woman outside the Sutton Book Club was headed straight toward them, her eyes to the horizon. In the deep distance, a ferry boat churned toward the harbor. *Was she meeting someone?*

"Hey! Rebecca?" Ben surprised himself by greeting her.

Rebecca turned her head. Her smile was reminiscent of Esme's, the kind that lit up a entire room. "Hi there." She made a beeline for them as, under his breath, Doug said, "Someone has a crush."

"Shush," Ben muttered to Doug.

"How are you two doing?" Rebecca asked.

"Just enjoying the sun," Ben said. "And yourself?"

Rebecca tilted her head as though she wasn't sure how to answer the question. "I don't know. My mother never came home the other night."

"Huh. That's bizarre."

"My father and I don't really know what to do about it. The police told us it wasn't our business, which is probably fair given my family's history."

Doug nodded slightly as though he agreed. "It's strange of her to close the Book Club. Then again, it must be hard on her to be there alone with Larry gone."

Rebecca's face was pained. "I'm sure she'll turn up." She pointed toward the ferry, adding, "My little sister is on that boat."

"Wow. The Suttons back together again." Although Doug was often sarcastic, he sounded genuinely surprised.

"Not all of us," Rebecca admitted sadly. "That would take a miracle."

Ben palmed the back of his neck. "I hope you find her soon."

"Me, too."

Ben spoke before he could think. "If you see her, could you ask her when the next Veterans' Dinner will be? I know a lot of us look forward to them."

The Veterans' Dinner was the only time Ben and Doug ate until they were full. It was the only time they felt relaxed around a group of peers who understood the most consequential events of their lives. It was true what they said about going to war—you were never the same afterward. And nobody really understood that without going through it themselves.

"I'll ask her." Rebecca frowned as though she suspected a darker truth behind Ben's question. "I better get to the ferry. I hope you enjoy the sun." She waved as she departed, fleeing toward the incoming boat.

"I hate to break it to you," Doug began as they headed back toward the truck, "but that beautiful woman was wearing a wedding ring. Somebody already scooped her up. Tough luck, Ben, my boy."

Ben chuckled. Doug could joke all he wanted about

Ben's dating life; the truth of it was, Ben felt like damaged goods. *How could anyone ever like him, let alone love him, after all he'd seen?*

"Let's head home," Ben said. "Before another woman breaks my heart."

Chapter Eleven

The ferry boat purred at the edge of the dock. Rebecca craned her neck to see Bethany somewhere in the crowd of tourists, her hands on the boardwalk railing to ensure she didn't topple into the water below. Around her, people clutched their suitcases and backpacks and discussed their recent vacation on the island, complaining of stomachaches and hangovers and jobs they would soon return to. Rebecca was prepared to tear through the crowd and throw her arms around her little sister. She was ready to embarrass herself in front of hundreds of strangers if it meant showing Bethany how much she still loved her.

Ever sensible, Bethany hung back from the violent crowd, waiting her turn to walk along the boardwalk. She wore a trench coat and a pair of sunglasses, and her hair looked blondish from the southern sun. Rebecca weaved through the throng of tourists, tears in her eyes, until she reached Bethany. There, she placed her hands on Bethany's elbows and gasped.

"You look so much like Mom," she whispered.

Bethany laughed gently. "You look just like her, too."

Perhaps they hadn't recognized this in their everyday reflections. They hadn't noticed, day after day, that their faces had transformed into their mother's face. But now that they stood before one another, they came to terms with how many years had passed—and how many years they couldn't get back. Wordless, Rebecca hugged her sister and closed her eyes. Her perfume was a heavenly cloud around them. By contrast, Rebecca had struggled to shower and dress herself that morning. Nantucket had really gotten the best of her.

Bethany grabbed her suitcase from the luggage rack and wheeled it behind her. Together, the two Sutton sisters collapsed into the crowd and headed toward the parking lot, where Rebecca's SUV waited. By the time the suitcase was stored in the back, Bethany's forehead was wrinkled with worry. "He was drunk. At the Sunset Cove Bar?"

Rebecca grimaced. "I've never seen him look like that. He was so broken. And he hasn't come out of the guest room all morning."

"And still no help from the police?"

Rebecca shook her head.

"Let's go to the station," Bethany stuttered. "I don't want to face Dad right now. It's just too much."

Rebecca locked the SUV, and together, the Sutton sisters traipsed across the parking lot toward the downtown police station. Bethany's head twitched as she took in the once-familiar sights and sounds of the island. "I can't believe we're really here," she breathed.

"Tell me about it. It's been like a nightmare ever since I arrived," Rebecca admitted. "And wait till you see your bedroom."

Bethany's jaw dropped. "It's the same?"

"Almost," Rebecca affirmed. "It's like a time capsule."

Rebecca didn't mention the room down the hall, the one Esme had kept like a museum. None of them had any right to go in there. Esme probably only entered to dust and vacuum, thus preserving the space, just as she always had. But this made Rebecca even more ashamed. She'd run off and built her own life. All the while, Esme had been stuck at home, ensuring that room remained the same. She hadn't been able to run from it.

The police station was a one-story red-brick building, and the officers inside were accustomed to simple tourist complaints and the occasional bar fight. Growing up on Nantucket had meant that "hard crime" was in another dimension.

Rebecca and Bethany greeted the woman at the front desk with matching smiles.

"Good afternoon! Are Franklin or Conner around?" Rebecca's voice was chipper.

"They are. What is this regarding?"

"A missing person," Bethany said forcefully. "The issue was not handled sufficiently yesterday, so we would like to address it further." She paused and locked eyes with Rebecca. "I am not afraid to take my worries off the island and get the state involved."

The woman at the front desk bristled. As she hurried off to find Franklin or Conner, Rebecca whispered, "That was intense."

Bethany shrugged. "I have to sound authoritative during surgery. It helps elsewhere sometimes."

Franklin and Conner returned to the front desk with the helpless-looking secretary. They eyed Bethany and Rebecca warily.

"Hello, Rebecca. Hello, Bethany." Conner crossed his arms over his chest. "I assume this means your mother hasn't come home?"

Rebecca stuttered. "Don't you think it's strange, Conner? Wouldn't you be worried if your mother hadn't come home for two days?"

"The fridge is fully stocked!" Bethany cried. Apparently, this detail had really stuck.

Franklin and Conner exchanged glances. Rebecca had a hunch the secretary had passed on Bethany's threat.

"We'll make some phone calls," Franklin said. "Leave your numbers here." He slid a pad of paper across the counter.

"Thank you," Bethany said, scowling as she scrawled her number. Rebecca followed suit.

Afterward, Bethany and Rebecca wandered the gorgeous streets of downtown Nantucket. They were quiet, their minds whirling. Bethany snuck into a corner store and bought a bottle of water, which she shared with Rebecca as they continued to walk. Rebecca was nervous that being on Nantucket would be too much for Bethany, and she would decide to leave later that day.

Before they knew what they'd done, they'd wandered to the Sutton Book Club. The old colonial stood on a patch of lush green grass, shrouded with ancient oaks and maples. The sign out front—the Sutton Book Club—had been set up by their Grandpa Thomas when they were children. He'd wanted the place to have his only grandchildren's last name. To Rebecca's memory, Grandpa Thomas had been thrilled with Victor as a son-in-law, so much so that they'd spent hours going over theoretical ideas and philosophical texts, usually deep into the night. Rebecca remembered listening to the murmur of their conversations through the walls.

"Have you been inside?" Bethany asked as they walked up the front porch.

"It was locked when we got here," Rebecca explained. She then dropped down to peer under the welcome mat. Sure enough, another set of keys glinted.

"Are you sure we should?" Bethany asked.

"Maybe there's a clue about where she went," Rebecca said, cursing herself for not looking before.

The Sutton Book Club was a three-story part library, part community center, part whatever Nantucket needed it to be. Their grandfather and then Esme had worked tirelessly to amass a monumental collection of books, most of which they checked out to the public. The front part of the first floor also served as a bookstore, where Esme sold Nantucket trinkets, paintings from local artists, and, of course, novels, nonfiction texts about Nantucket, poetry books, and so much more. As teenagers, the girls worked a few days a week at the bookstore in return for five dollars per hour. My, how times had changed.

The first story also housed a beautiful and well-lit all-purpose room with two long wooden tables and plenty of chairs. A café was open part-time and sold muffins, crois-sants, little cakes, tea, and coffee. Esme hosted reading clubs, music-listening clubs, theater-performing clubs, and the bi-monthly Veterans' Dinner. Rebecca felt a pang of guilt in memory of Ben and Doug. They seemed to need the Veterans' Dinner very much.

Bethany and Rebecca unlocked and entered the first story. Rebecca hunkered behind her little sister, grateful to lean on someone else's bravery for a change.

"It feels like she hasn't been gone long," Bethany said. "It's clean. Organized."

Rebecca nodded. "Let's check out the office upstairs."

Rebecca locked the door, then followed her sister to the staircase. Together, they crept to the second story, where thick and impenetrable books lined gorgeous hand-carved bookshelves. A desk on that level featured a traditional ledger, where Esme wrote the names of rented books alongside the renters' names. Rebecca read through the ledger, noting that Esme had just checked out a book three days before. Four weeks before, Larry had written his final check out.

The office had once belonged to Grandpa Thomas before he'd ultimately passed it on to Esme. Rebecca could remember when it had been a chaotic mess of World War II books, piles of envelopes, and Werther's candies, all heavy with the smell of Grandpa Thomas's cologne.

These days, Esme and Larry kept the office spick and span. They'd clearly shared it, as two cushioned chairs sat behind it—the king's and the queen's. A computer sat on the far right of the desk. Bethany turned it on, and Rebecca watched as it booted up, easing them into Esme and Larry's private technological world. They hadn't bothered with a passcode. This was Nantucket, after all.

Rebecca sat at the computer and searched through the Sutton Book Club's email for clues. Spam took up the majority of the space—coupons for groceries and historical texts. Bethany rifled through the desk drawers, reading old bills. Both were quiet for a long time.

"Oh my gosh."

Rebecca turned to find Bethany with a huge stack of handwritten letters. She spread them out across the desk, and her lips parted with surprise. "There are hundreds. And they're all from Mom to Larry or from Larry to Mom."

Rebecca stood beside her sister to inspect the letters. True to form, Esme wrote with exquisite cursive; her hand had complete control over the pen. Larry's handwriting was tighter and trimmer without as much flourish. Still, the way he wrote to their mother revealed a depth of thought and love that surprised them both.

Rebecca gasped and dropped back onto the chair. After a very long moment of silence, she said, "They were so in love."

Bethany's face was stricken. "She must be in tremendous pain."

Rebecca closed her eyes, thinking back to the first month after Fred's death. Without her children as anchors, she very well could have floated off into the stratosphere. *Where on earth was Esme?*

Rebecca returned her search to the computer, where she noticed a series of emails with the subject line: **Veterans' Dinner**. None of them had been addressed by anyone named Doug or Ben. Rather, it seemed a number of men and a few women in the area looked forward to the Veterans' Dinner and wondered when Esme planned to reinstate it. Rebecca allowed herself to open three of the emails from three different veterans. All three told Esme how sorry they were for her loss. One said, "You've been there for us during some of the darkest hours of our lives. Let us be there for you."

Resigned and hungry, Rebecca and Bethany locked up the Sutton Book Club and walked back to the SUV. It was nearly evening, and a chill clung to the air. Tourists skittered back to their hotel rooms to find sweaters and jackets. Bethany climbed into the passenger seat of the SUV and said, "I never thought I would come back here. I'm starting to wonder why."

"I've been thinking the same thing. We should have known Larry. We should have witnessed our mother happy."

"Especially after all she went through when we were teenagers," Bethany added.

Rebecca sighed as her phone buzzed. The area code was Nantucket's, so it was a local number.

"Hello?"

"Hi, Rebecca. It's Franklin." He sounded weak and jittery, which weren't the best attributes for a cop. "I wanted to let you know we've been in contact with your mother."

Rebecca's ears rang. "Where is she?"

"She said she's fine and not to worry."

Rebecca stuttered. "Yes, but where is she? When will she be back?"

Franklin was quiet. Beside Rebecca, Bethany gaped at her.

"To be honest, we only know this because she called my mother," Franklin backpedaled. "But my mother says Esme is taking care of an important matter and will be back soon."

Rebecca's jaw hung open. *What kind of police force was this?* Then again, she'd known Franklin and Conner since she was a kid. How could she have expected anything better?

"Okay. Thank you, I guess." Rebecca was at a loss. "I suppose your mother didn't tell my mother her daughters were here?"

"I'm sure she did," Franklin affirmed. "The gossip is

running like wildfire. But you know how Mrs. Walton is. She's called half the island."

After the call ended, Rebecca slowly removed her phone from her ear. Bethany gaped at her, expectant.

"What's going on?" Bethany demanded.

Rebecca's nostrils flared. "She knows we're here."

"And? Where is she? Is she coming back?"

Rebecca shrugged. "I don't know anything else." Listless, she shifted the car from park and slowly eased through the parking lot, heading back to the old Victorian home. It seemed as though both Victor and Esme were in the midst of a horrendous later-life crises as she dealt with her own midlife one. She prayed Bethany was up for the ride. They needed her.

Chapter Twelve

The mattress hadn't dried properly. This was a conundrum, as Doug had already nodded off in his chair in front of the television and would soon need a real place to sleep. Ben heaved his own mattress from his bed upstairs and walked down the stairs very slowly, careful not to trip. If he got injured, what would Doug do? When he reached the living room, he set the mattress into Doug's bed frame, stretched new sheets onto it, added fresh pillows, and clapped his hands. Doug peered at him sleepily from his chair.

"All this racket is distracting," he complained. "I'm trying to watch my shows."

"Don't lie to me. You're as exhausted as I am."

"Where the heck are you going to sleep?" Doug demanded. Slowly, he shifted forward in his chair and stood. The pain was apparent in his eyes, but he didn't complain.

"Don't worry about me. I'll figure something out," Ben explained.

Within the next ten minutes, Doug was fast asleep in the living room. Ben flipped off the television and turned his attention to his own needs. It was only nine at night, and his mind whirred with worries about the house. What he needed was a walk. What he needed was a drink.

Ben wasn't a big drinker. Riddled with trauma, sorrow, and PTSD, he was frightened that too much alcohol would throw him into a dark chasm of despair. As it was, he drank a beer here and there with Doug, who didn't seem to think twice about enjoying himself. Probably when you were ninety-eight, all your neuroses fell away. The future was no longer something to fear.

Ben placed Doug's cell phone directly beside Doug's bed, along with a note to call him if he needed anything. He then tugged on his spring jacket, donned a black beanie, and headed into the crisp June night.

The moon hung low in the pitch-black sky, and stars sparkled over their little island in the middle of the ocean. For not the first time, Ben asked himself if Nantucket was real or if he'd invented it somewhere in his traumatized mind. As he walked toward Sunset Cove Bar, he watched the tourists. Wearing a gentle smile, he observed fathers carrying their tired children on their chests, older children licking ice cream cones, and mothers pushing strollers, their eyes soft with fatigue and happiness.

What would it have been like to feel like a part of a family? Would Ben have liked to be a father? To feel responsible for helpless little children? Sometimes, Ben had dreams about his ex-wife. In the dreams, he'd never gone to war, and they'd had children. The dreams were filled with small arguments, laughing fits in a kitchen he didn't recognize, and long walks through a city he'd never seen before. By the time he awoke, his psyche had nearly convinced him his dreams were true.

The Sunset Cove Bar was jam-packed. Only one barstool remained at the bar counter, and Ben made a beeline for it. It was better that the bar was busy; it meant nobody would single him out and wonder why he was all alone.

Ben ordered a beer and looked at his phone for a little while. Due to his poor attendance because of his depression last summer, he hadn't been asked back to his dishwashing job, which left him in a bind. He scanned through online applications for other dishwasher, server, and deliverer positions and sent a few inquiries. As usual when he applied anywhere, he knew the next job would go nowhere. They would fire him sooner or later, and he would have to find another to take its place.

And eventually, his and Doug's house would crumble around them. They would be homeless veterans. Just another statistic.

Disheartened, Ben ordered another beer and glanced around the bar, careful not to linger on anyone too long. If he didn't want anyone to stare at him, he couldn't stare back.

That was when he noticed him. Rebecca's father, who'd been outside the Sutton Book Club, sat two stools away. He was hunched over his beer, and his gray hair spilled wildly around his ears. He muttered to himself and cupped his ears.

As Ben watched, another older man approached. His voice boomed over the chaos of other conversations. "Is that you, Victor Sutton?"

Victor turned to show panicked eyes. After a split

second, he took back control of his face. "Henry Collins. You son of a gun." They clapped hands and shook.

The stool between Ben and Victor had recently been vacated. Henry slid onto it and shook his head at Victor. "I never thought I'd see the day you'd walk back through the doors of the Sunset Cove."

"It's your lucky day. Or is it your nightmare?" Victor tried to laugh, but it sounded all wrong.

"I see you on television all the time," Henry continued. "The world-renowned family and child psychologist. What you did with that talk show host last year was monumental. At least, that's what my wife calls it."

Victor grunted. From what Ben could see, all the light had drained from his eyes.

"My wife told me Esme's missing," Henry went on. "But half the island thinks she's just hiding out until you leave." Henry wheezed with laughter.

Victor tried to join him yet failed.

"We came to really like Larry," Henry continued. "Good man. Like Esme, he was all about that Book Club. I remember Esme saying you only read something if it furthered your career. Oh, but heck. Your career is far and away better than anyone else's around here. I guess all that reading paid off."

Ben's heart dropped into his stomach. *Who was this horrible man? And why did he feel it necessary to kick Victor when he was obviously down?*

Suddenly, Ben did something he hardly ever did. He meddled in someone else's business.

Ben tapped Henry's shoulder. Henry turned his head quickly as Ben peered around him to find Victor. "There you are, Mr. Sutton! I've been looking around for you everywhere. Come to find out, you're just two seats to the right."

At first, Victor's eyes were dim. He didn't recognize Ben at all. Victor probably thought he just wanted to dig into his private business as Henry did.

Ben looked at Henry, who was quizzical. "I'm dear friends with Victor's daughter, Rebecca. I have something important to discuss with him. If you don't mind?"

It took Henry a split second to get the hint. He saluted Victor, then Ben, and stepped back from the stool. "Of course. Let me know when your private meeting is through. I'd love a little more time to catch up with my dear friend." As Ben eased onto the stool beside him, he patted Victor's shoulder again.

With Henry gone, Ben sipped his beer and remained silent.

Under his breath, Victor coughed, "Thanks for getting me out of that."

"If I understand anything, it's wanting to be left alone."

For a long time, Victor and Ben were quiet. They sipped beers slowly, looked at their phones, and allowed the minutes to tick past. Around them, the bar grew increasingly volatile, then quieted. Someone sitting next to Victor without speaking was better than sitting at the bar alone.

Victor cleared his throat. Ben glanced around to see that one half of the bar had cleared. Henry was nowhere to be found.

"You're the young veteran we met the other day outside the Sutton Book Club," he said.

Ben nodded.

"I don't suppose you've heard anything from Esme since then?"

"I'm afraid not. But I can't imagine I'd be first on her list to reach out to."

Victor sipped his beer. "Two of my daughters are back at the house. They told me Esme's been in contact with someone on the island. She knows we're here, but she's choosing to stay away." He coughed. "I can't blame her."

Ben felt very cold. By contrast with the man beside him, he'd never known the kind of familiar love that could cast such a long shadow of resentment.

"Esme's your ex-wife?" Ben asked.

Victor nodded. "We've been divorced for many years." After another pause, he asked, "Want to know how many of those years I regretted leaving her?"

Ben was surprised at how open Victor was with him, a stranger. "How many?"

"All of them," Victor affirmed.

Ben was wordless. In the corner, someone messed with the jukebox and played a Simon and Garfunkel song, one Ben's mother had loved.

"Can I ask why you did it?" Ben asked softly.

Victor sniffed. For a moment, Ben thought for sure he'd gone too far. He hated, for example, when people asked him why he'd joined the service in the first place. There was only so much about the past you could explain.

"Things got really bad," Victor said. "Despite coming together during a horrific time, Esme and I became strangers. One morning, after I'd spent all night crying in my office, I slept with my assistant, Bree. The affair got out of hand. And before I knew it, I'd taken a position at the University of Rhode Island, and Bree and I were off to the races with our brand-new life."

Victor told the story as though he spoke about someone else's life. Ben's heart hammered. He burned with questions, none of which he felt confident enough to ask. Instead, he allowed Victor to recede back into his thoughts, safe with Ben beside him to carry whatever he needed to share.

Chapter Thirteen

The morning after Bethany's arrival, the two Sutton sisters sat together at the breakfast table and tried to call Esme's phone again. It rang and rang and rang until it finally cut to voicemail, at which time Rebecca sent a message.

Mom. It's Rebecca and Bethany. We really need to speak to you. Will you call us back?

Bethany poured them cups of coffee and blew at the steam. She wore no makeup, and Rebecca studied the soft wrinkles around her mouth and the crow's feet that deepened around her eyes. Her wrinkles seemed the same.

"Did you hear Dad come in last night?" Bethany asked.

"Around one?"

"Yeah." Bethany shook her head softly. "What was he up to?"

"He's a grown man. I guess he can take care of himself?" Rebecca hesitated, unsure if she believed herself. "How did it feel to see him yesterday?"

"It felt like getting run over by a truck," Bethany

admitted. "When he hugged me, it reminded me of that last day before he left. Remember? When he told us he was moving to Rhode Island with Bree."

Rebecca shivered at the memory. Esme had remained upstairs, unwilling to watch her husband hug his kids for the last time.

"He asked me questions about my kids. About my husband. And it just made me think about all the years we've missed as a family. We should have all been together." Bethany sipped her coffee. "And then I went to the kitchen to pour myself a glass of wine, and when I got back to the living room, he was gone. Off to God knows where."

"He has no idea how to process his feelings about being back," Rebecca stated. "Not that I do, either."

"Here's to being a Sutton. Whatever that means." Bethany raised her coffee mug.

A little while later, Rebecca remembered her mother's address book. It sat on the phone table in the living room, where it had been for decades. She hurried to fetch it, then found Franklin's mother's phone number. According to the police officers, she was the only person who'd had contact with Esme.

"Hello?" an older woman's voice answered.

"Mrs. Sanderson? It's Rebecca Sutton." Rebecca smiled into the phone, hoping she sounded friendly.

"Oh! Rebecca!" Franklin's mother seemed ecstatic. Probably, she was grateful to be in the very center of the Sutton gossip. "I heard a rumor you were back. And you're calling from your mother's house!"

"That's right." Rebecca eyed Bethany, suddenly nervous. "I heard you spoke with my mother."

"I did. A marvelous woman, your mother. We'll be friends till the end."

Rebecca recognized a wall when she saw one. Mrs. Sanderson would protect Esme at all costs. *But why?* She rubbed her temple and added, "I've been trying to call her all morning."

"I imagine she's quite busy."

Rebecca smiled wider, frustrated. "She is a remarkable woman. So busy. Always five steps ahead of everyone else."

"I feel the same!"

Rebecca's eyes bugged out. "Did she mention when she was heading back to the island?"

Mrs. Sanderson stuttered. "I can't imagine she'll be long now."

"Right. Because she wouldn't leave the Sutton Book Club for so long."

Mrs. Sanderson made a strange noise in her throat.

"Right?" Rebecca asked.

"Sure, honey. I'm sure you know your mother best." Her voice shimmered with sarcasm.

Annoyed, Rebecca said her goodbyes and hung up. Bethany gave her an inquisitive smile. "That didn't sound promising."

"It's like the whole island is working against us," Rebecca said. "Like we're an infection they're trying to fight off."

Rebecca explained that Mrs. Sanderson thought Esme would probably be back soon. Bethany looked thoughtful.

"How long do you have before you need to go home?" Rebecca asked.

"I have time," Bethany explained. She gestured

around them and down the hallway toward the guest room. Under her breath, she added, "I want to make sure they're both stable before I go."

Rebecca's stomach tightened with sorrow. It suddenly occurred to her that the "reunion" would probably feel lackluster once Esme returned. How could the Sutton family possibly translate so many years of sorrows, fears, and reflections in a single afternoon? And what would happen afterward? Victor no longer had Bree. Rebecca no longer had Fred. They would hang their heads and return to other parts of the country, defeated.

Bethany had to make some phone calls to the hospital to check on her patients. This left Rebecca to wade sullenly through the kitchen and her childhood bedroom at a loss. She texted Lily, Shelby, and Chad for updates, and no one responded. She cursed herself for being so needy.

Rebecca donned a pair of shorts, a light sweatshirt, and her running shoes and stepped into the late morning light. For years, she'd used running to calm her anxiety around motherhood and being a head chef. All it took, usually, was thirty minutes. Fred had called it her "therapy." Sometimes, they'd run together, racing across Maine beaches and up mountain trails. It seemed odd that Fred had been so healthy, only to die in such a stupid way.

No. She couldn't think about Fred. Not now.

Rebecca began to jog down the beach. The sand fought her, trying to eat her shoes. When exhaustion took hold of her, she turned back to the streets and headed downtown to loop through the old-world colonial buildings and people-watch. Other joggers passed her and waved as though they belonged to one community.

Yet again, Rebecca found herself in front of the

Sutton Book Club. It was still locked up, and the curtains pulled to shield the older books from the sharp sun rays. Grandpa Thomas had always said it was up to them to protect the older books from damage. They were relics of history.

Rebecca turned back toward the beach. Her muscles felt electric and recharged, and her thoughts felt zippy and fast. When she finally staggered back out onto the sand, she gripped her waist and lifted her face to take in the full splendor of the sun. To ground herself back in reality, she considered the current facts of her life. Number one: she was on Nantucket Island. Number two: her mother was not missing; she was just taking her time to come home. Number three: her love for Bethany was powerful. Already, it had given her a newfound strength, one she hadn't felt since before Fred's death.

As Rebecca walked down the beach, she spotted two familiar figures. She stopped, placed her hand over her forehead, and took them in—a very old man and a muscular young man, both stretched out on a blanket as the sun warmed them and the waves cascaded toward shore.

Rebecca's heart seized with a mix of sorrow and wonder. As she approached them, she tried to imagine the story of how Ben and Doug had met one another. *What had led a young man in his forties to live his life with a very old man?*

"Hi there." Rebecca waved as she approached.

Ben leaped up with surprise. Doug adjusted his hat and laughed good-naturedly. It was the kind of laughter that wrapped around you and warmed your soul.

"I knew this island was small," Rebecca continued. "You troublemakers seem to pop up everywhere."

Ben laughed. He seemed oddly embarrassed or very shy. "You're out for a run?"

"That's right," Rebecca said. "But the sand is exhausting."

Ben nodded. Rebecca suddenly thought that Ben's war had been fought in the Middle Eastern desert, so he probably knew more about sand than just about anyone.

"We're having a picnic." Ben gestured to a brown paper sack.

"Ben makes a mighty fine bologna and cheese sandwich," Doug boasted.

"I'm sure that's nothing to you. Your dad told me you're a chef." Ben smiled nervously.

Rebecca tilted her head. *When had Ben spent any time with her father?*

"I ran into him at the bar last night," Ben added. The glint in his eyes told Rebecca there was more to the story than he was willing to share.

"I hope he was okay?"

"He was fine," Ben said. "Neither of us could sleep last night. We kept each other company."

"Ben makes me go to bed early," Doug explained. "Do you think I should claim elder abuse?" He cackled with laughter as Ben swatted him playfully.

Rebecca laughed gently, unsure of what to say. *Had Victor revealed all of the Suttons' dirty laundry? Did Ben know everything? Then again, if he did, was that so bad?* Their dirty laundry was practically ancient at this point.

"You should sit with us," Doug suggested. "You're making me nervous up there."

Rebecca dropped onto the warm sand beside Doug. Doug leafed through a brown paper bag and removed a Budweiser and passed it over to her, pressing his finger to his lips. "Don't tell the young one I'm drinking this early in the afternoon. He gets finicky."

Rebecca accepted the beer but didn't open it. Doug's eyes glittered happily as he sipped his brew and gazed out across the water. Probably, he had a better idea of how to appreciate the beauty of the day than she did.

"She'll come back," Ben said suddenly, surprising Rebecca. "Esme, I mean. She's a Nantucketer, through and through. She wouldn't know what to do with herself anywhere else."

Rebecca sighed. She hoped Ben was right. "She seemed happy with Larry?"

"Over the moon," Doug affirmed. "She blushed like a schoolgirl when Larry was around."

Rebecca's heart lifted. Again, she was grateful her mother had been able to fall in love again after so many years of darkness.

"Larry was a young one," Doug continued. "At ninety-eight, it's strange to see such young men pass. You wonder what the rules of the world are."

Rebecca eyed him. "Then again, you were in World War II. I imagine you've lived with those thoughts for eighty years."

Doug continued to watch the water. "Every war is senseless. The men who fought valiantly beside me should have returned just the same as me." He tilted his head toward Ben to add, "There's no reason we should still be alive. But since we are, we have to live with the consequences of being veterans. It's not always easy."

Ben's eyes were clouded. Again, Rebecca remembered the emails the Sutton Book Club had received from veterans across the island, anxious to return for Veterans' Night.

She was a chef, and the Sutton Book Club had a working kitchen. The key was underneath the front mat.

What was she waiting for? Why couldn't she host a Veterans' Dinner by herself?

In turn, wouldn't that prove to Esme how much Rebecca still cared for the Sutton Book Club and, subsequently, the Sutton family?

"Do you have plans tomorrow afternoon?" Rebecca asked.

Doug bucked with laughter and sipped his beer.

"He means to say we never have plans," Ben joked. "What did you have in mind?"

Rebecca furrowed her brow. "Veterans' Dinner is back on. I'll send an email out. Make sure anyone who doesn't have email gets the message. Okay?"

As Rebecca fled home, her heart lifted into her throat. Seagulls cawed overhead and swept low to the earth, casting their shadows across the sands. The ground no longer threatened to swallow her up. Instead, she ran with what seemed like endless power.

Chapter Fourteen

Rebecca returned home to find Bethany on the back porch with a book. Her hair fluttered with the sea breeze, and her relaxed face remained stoic. As Rebecca leaped up the back steps, Bethany stretched her arms over her head and said, "I haven't had such a relaxing morning in years. Decades, even."

Rebecca smiled and removed her hair tie. Her hair dropped along her arms and back, and sweat lined her back. Euphoric from the run, she said, "I'm just so glad to see you again, Bethany."

Bethany placed her book on the table and smiled gently at Rebecca. "What's gotten into you?"

Rebecca laughed and collapsed into the chair across from her. She explained her plan for the Sutton Book Club in a few sentences. "On the run back, I planned the whole menu. It's the first time I've been excited about cooking since Fred passed away."

"Then we have to do it," Bethany affirmed. "Tell me how I can help."

First thing, they had to return to the Sutton Book Club to send a mass email to the veterans Esme had listed on her computer. Next, Rebecca inspected the kitchen, which she found subpar when compared to the kitchen she'd left behind in Bar Harbor. "It'll have to do," she said.

Before they headed home, Rebecca checked the computer again. Already, four veterans had RSVPed.

Rebecca and Bethany walked home, chatting gently about the groceries Rebecca needed to shop for. Bethany mentioned that Victor had told her about Rebecca's "impeccable" cooking skills, and Rebecca blushed. "Dad seems to be telling that to everyone around town," she said. She then explained she'd run into Ben. "He ran into Dad at the bar last night."

"You're kidding." Bethany bowed her head. "This island is something else."

"I think it turned out to be a good thing. Ben was able to watch out for him." Rebecca noticed how eager she'd been to bring Ben up in conversation. His name burned on her tongue. "Ben is around our age, I guess, but he lives with that very old veteran named Doug. Do you remember him?"

Bethany's jaw dropped. "He's still alive?" She then snapped her hand over her mouth, ashamed.

"I know. He seemed so old when we were kids," Rebecca said. "I have a hunch neither of them is doing so well. Ben mentioned the Veterans' Dinner is a very important event on their monthly calendar."

"Strange, isn't it? We're told the troops are the most incredible blessings, but so many of them struggle after they serve." Bethany shook her head. "Remember how Mom used to talk about Grandpa? He always slept-walked, and Grandma was terrified to wake him up because he always thought he was back in the war."

Rebecca had forgotten. She stopped at a crosswalk and allowed the story to sink in. It seemed incredible that so many people still remained on earth with memories of World War II. She'd just spoken to Doug that day, watching as he'd engaged with yet another day in a long history of his days. *Was he still grateful for each of them?*

Back at home, they were surprised to find Victor Sutton in the kitchen. Dark shadows were beneath his eyes, and he wore a pair of jeans and a T-shirt. He'd filled a glass with water, and he searched their faces curiously, as though he'd woken up without memory of the few days before.

"Hi, Dad." Rebecca smiled.

Bethany was quiet.

"Where did you run off to?" Victor sounded groggy.

"We went to the Book Club," Rebecca explained. "The veterans in Nantucket really look forward to their dinners. I've decided to hold one tomorrow night."

Victor's eyes sparkled with intrigue. "That's quite an idea." After a long pause, he palmed the back of his neck and added, "How can I help?"

Bethany and Rebecca eyed one another. This was the strangest trio the world had ever seen.

"I have the menu planned," Rebecca began.

"I have no doubt about that." He again eyed Bethany to say, "She really is a stunning cook."

Rebecca nodded toward Bethany. "I could never do what she does, though. Surgery? Dad, can you even imagine? She must be the bravest of us all."

"My brainiac," Victor affirmed sadly.

Bethany looked nervous. She filled a glass with water

and looked out the window, unaccustomed to their father's compliments. Rebecca understood the weight of them. After so many years without his feedback, it felt like too much.

"I'll practice tonight," Rebecca suggested. "It's been weeks since I cooked anything and many months since I've cooked anything without freaking out."

"You don't have to do that," Bethany tried.

But Rebecca was resolute. "Just let me cook for you, Bethany. You said yourself you've finally been able to relax here on Nantucket. I'm sure you have to cook and clean for your husband and kids all the time."

Bethany grimaced. "Cooking a full dinner isn't my favorite thing to do after surgery."

"Not surprised about that." She gave Bethany a firm smile, an attempt to let Bethany know she had everything under control. She was the big sister, after all. After that, Rebecca rushed around, writing a list of groceries for the night. Victor and Bethany watched her, bemused. Rebecca again had the sensation that if she moved quickly, her sorrows couldn't catch up with her. If she cared for everyone else, the world would spin, just as it always had.

* * *

The evening sky was lavender, speckled with birds and beach kites. On the back porch, Bethany and Victor sat with optimistic eyes, watching as Rebecca heaved a large platter of an Indian fish curry to the table. Curry spices simmered in the air.

"My goodness!" Bethany cried.

Rebecca's heart was full. She gripped her wineglass

tentatively and watched as her father and sister took their first bites. With their eyes closed, they gave themselves over to the buttery sauce and the decadent texture. Rebecca knew their expressions. She'd seen the same ones across the dining room at Bar Harbor Brasserie.

"Rebecca," Bethany whispered. "I remember when we were teenagers, and you cooked little things for us. You were good! Especially for a sixteen-year-old. But I never could have imagined you'd become this extraordinary chef."

"I was fascinated with the cooking process back then," Rebecca admitted. "But I had absolutely no technique."

"You loved to eat, though," Bethany said with a laugh. "We all did."

"Three teenage girls with crazy appetites," Rebecca affirmed.

Across from her, Victor twitched nervously. Rebecca and Bethany had entered stories from an era he hadn't been involved in. By the time Rebecca had begun to cook for the family, he'd already begun his new life with Bree. A part of Rebecca ached to ask him about Bree, about the life he'd built with her, but another part felt the questions were like daggers.

Instead, it was better to exist in this strange and liminal space. According to gossip, Esme would return home soon. Rebecca prayed the upcoming Veterans' Dinner would call her back sooner. She prayed that soon, as a family, they could go over the events of their lives and finally make sense of them. It didn't mean they would ever have the kind of love other families took for granted. But maybe they would find a way to move forward... without hate.

* * *

Nantucket's fish market had a similar flair to Bar Harbor's. The next morning around six, Rebecca and Bethany wandered the fish stalls, greeted the fishermen, assessed the lobsters, and sipped piping-hot coffees as they watched the sunrise filter across the water. As they loaded fish in ice-filled coolers, Bethany handled the slimy bodies with ease.

"I was going to comment on how good you are with the fish," Rebecca began, "but then I remembered you're a surgeon. Nothing probably freaks you out."

"I've seen a lot in my line of work," Bethany agreed as she closed the cooler. "A bunch of big, goopy fish eyes don't scare me."

"What does scare you?" Rebecca asked. She slipped into the driver's seat of the SUV and eyed Bethany curiously.

Bethany sighed. "As a mother, the answer is easy."

Rebecca's stomach twisted into knots. She knew Bethany's answer; perhaps she'd already known it when she'd asked the question. "Yeah. I worry about mine constantly."

"How are they handling Fred's death?" Bethany asked.

"As well as can be expected." Rebecca turned on the engine and drove them away from the fish market and back toward the Sutton Book Club. "Sometimes, I think they're much more resilient than I am."

"That's the nature of being young, isn't it? It's so much easier to learn and grow and change."

Rebecca nodded, thinking of Lily in her apartment in Brooklyn, of Shelby in the Acadia Mountains, and Chad at basketball camp in Virginia. How she ached for them. How she wished they would tell her exactly what was on their minds. If she had the capacity to fix their broken hearts, she would. She would do anything.

To Rebecca's surprise, Victor arrived at the Sutton Book Club at four that afternoon. She and Bethany had just begun to slice and dice vegetables and prep the fish. They hadn't expected their father until dinnertime, if he bothered to show at all.

"Dad!" Rebecca greeted him with a side hug. As he walked into the Sutton Book Club, he eyed the downstairs bookstore, the antique staircase, and the beautiful paintings of Nantucket's coastlines and lighthouses.

"This place hasn't changed so much on the inside," he said timidly.

"Are you okay to be my sous chef? I need all the help I can get."

Victor followed Rebecca through the door that separated the community area and its two long wooden tables with the kitchen. A Bluetooth speaker played music from the eighties and nineties, which reminded Rebecca and Bethany of the years they'd spent together on Nantucket. Some of the songs were so emotional that memories threatened to make them break down. Still, they had a job to do. Fish had to be prepped and seasoned, salads prepared, and onions sliced. Throughout, they sang the lyrics they remembered and made up the ones they didn't.

Rebecca set Victor up with a sharp knife, onions, peppers, eggplant, and garlic. Victor set his jaw, clearly nervous. He wanted to please Rebecca. As he began, it struck Rebecca that Chad had many of her father's facial features. *Why had she never noticed before? Had they been in the same generation, they could have been twins.*

Victor was a crater in her family's story. But he did not hide from what he'd done. Perhaps he was in her mother's Book Club to ask for forgiveness. Maybe he was here to make amends.

The veterans began to arrive around five thirty. Bethany greeted them with warm smiles, and Victor waited for them in the dining area with tea and coffee, various types of juice, Coke products, and water. Rebecca remained in the sizzling madness of the kitchen, hyper-focused on the meal.

And suddenly, out of nowhere, Ben popped into the kitchen. Rebecca leaped with surprise, and she dropped a spatula on the floor. It bounced toward him.

"Oh no!" Ben laughed and got to the spatula before she could. He had the tap running in the sink and had scrubbed the spatula clean in no time. Suds covered his hands.

"You don't have to do that," Rebecca said. Her chest was hot, and her heart fluttered. She couldn't help but notice the powerful surge of Ben's arm muscles as he dried the spatula and handed it back to her.

"I didn't mean to frighten you," Ben reported. "I would have never just walked in here to say hello to Esme. I don't know what came over me."

Rebecca laughed and returned to the food on the stovetop. She had absolutely no idea what to say.

"It smells insanely good in here," Ben said.

"Thank you. I hope it turns out okay. I used to be good at cooking for a hundred people a night, but I'm out of practice."

"The most I've ever cooked for is two. Doug has made

it very clear he doesn't want me to get too experimental. A fish stew I tried a few years ago made us both sick." Ben chuckled.

Rebecca turned and locked eyes with Ben. She burned to know why he lived with Doug and had never settled with someone. He was a handsome veteran— strong, capable, and charming. Still, he had darkness behind his eyes, telling her there was more to the story than could meet the eye. He'd clearly seen active duty because a part of his soul had been destroyed.

"If you ever want some hints," Rebecca tried. "I'm not the world's best teacher, but I would be happy to give you a few lessons. To me, being able to cook a good meal is the single greatest gift you can give yourself."

"I imagine it's a different feeling than removing a frozen pizza from the oven," Ben joked.

Rebecca giggled. "Oh, but I have some decent tricks for frozen pizza. They don't always have to taste like cardboard."

Ben's smile was exceedingly handsome, so much so that Rebecca had to turn back to her food. For a moment, she thought she'd ruined the potatoes on the stovetop. She couldn't let herself get distracted. The veterans on Nantucket looked forward to this dinner. It had to be tremendous.

Bethany had set the two tables with twenty-two place settings. Along the far wall by the window, they'd decided to set up the buffet, so their guests could fill their plates with whatever they wanted. As Rebecca hurried out to the buffet table with an enormous basin of herb-crusted fish, Victor poured wine and passed out beers in the corner. She winked at him and mouthed, "Thank you." He just smiled back, at ease.

Ben hurried behind her, carrying the potatoes.

"They put you to work?" Doug stood near the table with a beer. He smiled eagerly and leaned on his cane with his other hand.

"They said I have to work for my dinner," Ben joked.

"That's right, Miss Rebecca. You have to keep him in line," Doug said. "I won't always be around to make sure he behaves."

Rebecca laughed and followed Ben back into the kitchen, where he collected two enormous bowls of salads. Rebecca grabbed the chopped watermelon and hurried out to the table. The guests were restless; they needed to eat. Bethany chatted with two women in their forties or fifties, both of whom had been stationed in Iraq. Rebecca heard bits and pieces of their conversation as she breezed in and out of the kitchen. "It was difficult to leave my children behind," one woman said. "My husband accused me of not being a proper mother, which was hard to hear. I'd trained in the military for years, just as he had, and I wanted to serve my country." Bethany nodded and furrowed her brow. Under her breath, she said, "That must have been so hard to hear."

Rebecca's heart seized with empathy for these women. It was one thing to love your children with all your heart and mind; it was another to ensure you lived a fulfilling life. Very few women in the world managed to do both. She supposed she was one of the lucky ones.

Chapter Fifteen

Rebecca was lucky to be seated in the middle of one of the long wooden tables. Beside her sat Bethany, and Victor was a few chairs down. Doug and Ben sat across from her. Now that she'd spent a bit more time with them, they resembled college roommates. All they did was pick on each other. All they did was find new and creative ways to tease.

"Didn't anyone ever tell you to grow up?" Rebecca asked Doug. Her fork was heavy with herb-crusted salmon, and she took a bite, then closed her eyes. Laughter and flavor bubbled through her. It was remarkable bliss.

"Doug's been on the run from growing up his entire life," Ben reported.

"Don't even get us started," another veteran down the table said. "Doug's been causing trouble around Nantucket for years."

Doug looked mischievous. "Nantucket in the sixties was a wild time. I'll tell you that."

Rebecca and Bethany locked eyes. "I think we need to hear more," Bethany urged.

"This is absolutely delectable, by the way, Rebecca," Doug said hurriedly, pointing his fork at the plate.

Rebecca blushed as Bethany cried, "Don't compliment your way out of telling us your stories."

"Oh great. Now you've given him an audience, and he won't shut up all night long," Ben joked. His eyes were alight as he bent across the table and added, under his breath, "This really is delicious, Rebecca. You have an incredible talent."

Rebecca's laughter echoed from wall-to-wall of the gorgeous space. Around them, other veterans swapped stories from years gone by, ate heartily, and filled their plates with fish, potatoes, freshly baked rolls, brussels sprouts, sweet potatoes, and crab cakes. Rebecca had gone all-out, and their contented eyes told her she'd succeeded. It was a spectacular feeling.

For the next few minutes, Doug pieced together a few of his stories from the sixties. Back then, apparently, he'd been married to "the most beautiful woman in all of Nantucket," but she'd left him for his very best friend and moved to Martha's Vineyard. "But I wasn't single for long," he explained. "The sixties were a time of optimism. Of change! And women were suddenly telling you what they wanted. I met a beautiful journalist named Gwen, and boy, did our lives take off after that." His eyes swam with nostalgia.

"Did you marry her?" Bethany asked.

"Of course. No matter what this clown tells you, I am and have always been a gentleman," Doug said. "We were married in a beach ceremony in 1965, and we went on to have three children."

Rebecca's lips parted with surprise. *Why had she assumed Doug had no children? That he was alone? But then again, where were those children and grandchildren? Why was Ben the only one around to care for him?*

But before Rebecca could ask any additional questions, Doug tilted his head and eyed her. "You know, I fought with your granddaddy in the war."

The table quieted. Every war was revered among veterans, and World War II rocked history in the greatest way.

"I knew you were in World War II," Rebecca breathed. "But I didn't know you fought with my grandpa Thomas."

"My God." Bethany shook her head.

Victor leaned forward, trying to involve himself in their conversation. "Doug, you used to tell a story from those days. Something about a German village? A dance?" His eyes sparkled at the memory.

Doug bucked with laughter. "Your grandfather and I were young men. Although we were starving and at war, we thought we were the strongest of all. We were stationed outside a village near Dortmund, and it was threateningly cold. Maybe ten or fifteen degrees. Thomas and I went for a little walk through the campsite as a way to warm our toes. That was when we saw them."

Rebecca was captivated. "Who?"

"Three young German women," Doug continued. "They were around our age, all bundled up in coats, hats, and mittens. They'd just been ice skating on a local pond. For whatever reason, they weren't afraid of us. One of them came over and asked to try on our hats. She hardly spoke any English, but we knew enough German by then to make it work."

Rebecca and Bethany shivered with laughter. Rebecca could practically feel the sharp chill of the German winter.

"Of course, Thomas and I were immediately smitten," Doug admitted with a grin. "The flirting warmed us up. But we were scared one of our officers would see us and cause trouble, so we asked to see them later. They told us to sneak out of camp that night and come to their village. I still remember. They drew us a map so we could find the way.

"That night, Thomas and I stayed up shivering in our tents. When it was clear, we raced out from the campsite, across three hills, left at the stream, and then onward until we found Scherfede. We could hear the music coming through the trees. It was just about the most magical sound I'd ever heard."

"But you were American soldiers," Bethany whispered. "Weren't you scared they would hurt you?"

"In those small villages, the Germans were more curious about us than anything," Doug explained. "When we appeared outside the dance hall, a man came to offer us two beers. He laughed and said things we didn't comprehend, so we laughed and thanked him and tried to make him understand we came in peace. By then, all Thomas and I wanted to do was come home to Nantucket. We wanted the war to be over. We wanted to see our families again. We wanted to live long enough to become real men.

"Anyway. The girls were there, just as they'd said they would be. And the prettiest of the three of them walked right up to your grandfather and asked him to dance. I swam with jealousy and took the next prettiest one. Mine was a spectacular dancer, though. Although I was starving and tired from months at war, I kept up with her and found myself laughing all night long." Doug looked wistful. He took a bite of potatoes and chewed slowly.

"You forgot to tell them who was dancing with their grandfather," Victor chimed in.

Doug's face brightened. "That's right. I forgot the best part of the story. The woman who marched up to your grandfather was the woman who ultimately changed his life forever. She was your grandmother, Rose."

Rebecca's jaw dropped. Bethany's face was the same.

"Why have we never heard that story?" Rebecca demanded.

But Rebecca already knew the answer. Grandma Rose died when Esme was young, so talking about Rose was painful. It drove both Esme and Grandpa Thomas into deep depressions. She hadn't lived long enough to give Esme any siblings, so for years, it had just been Thomas and Esme.

Doug's eyes were damp. He sipped his coffee while he toyed with a napkin. "All right. That's enough of that story. Don't let this old man bore you too much."

"That story was anything but boring," Rebecca said.

"Maybe, if you hang around Nantucket a little bit longer, I can share a few more," Doug added.

"We would like that." Rebecca's gaze went to her plate, suddenly too anxious to eat. "You must have been around when Grandpa Thomas opened the Sutton Book Club."

"I was around before it was ever called Sutton." Doug laughed. "Although I understand why he wanted to name it after his grandchildren's last name. He loved you children so much."

"When did you start coming to the Book Club?" Rebecca asked Ben.

Ben thought for a moment. "I came to Nantucket about five years ago and discovered the Veterans' Dinner about six months after that. Your grandfather and mother have created such a remarkable space here. Your mother has even conned me into reading some of the books."

"Only took him eight months to read *Moby Dick*," Doug joked.

"Two months, Doug. Two!" Ben blushed.

"That's not a thin book," Bethany affirmed.

"Thank you," Ben said. "Now that Doug's read just about every book ever written, he spends his days belittling my intelligence."

Doug bounced his elbow against Ben's upper arm as the table laughed.

After dinner, Rebecca and Bethany served cherry and apple pie and chocolate cake with icing. Their guests ate the cake on paper plates and continued to chat about the upcoming summer and their plans for picnics, hikes, and sailing adventures. Rebecca paused in the kitchen with a stack of dirty dinner plates to take a breath, and Bethany breezed through the door to say, "Mom would be so proud of you."

Rebecca turned to find Bethany near tears. Rebecca pressed her hand over her chest. A moment later, they met in the middle of the kitchen and hugged, both lost in the onslaught of their memories. So many years ago, amid a horrific war, their grandfather and grandmother met each other in the German snow. It was the only reason either of them stood in that kitchen today. It was the only reason their children existed.

Around nine thirty that night, the last of the veterans

lingered. They sipped coffee, cracked final jokes, and complimented Rebecca's cooking. Ben and Doug donned spring jackets and headed for the front door.

"I hope you'll let us know when Esme gets back to town," Ben said. "Maybe we can have a picnic on the beach together."

From the second-story window, Rebecca and Bethany waved to Ben and Doug. Ben slowed the truck down as Doug gave a firm wave.

Suddenly, Victor's voice boomed behind them. "What you did here tonight was remarkable."

Rebecca and Bethany turned to address their father. After hours of community, they now found themselves alone with heaps of dishes to wash and tons of bottles to recycle. Victor's smile was soft and tired, and he looked at his daughters with all the love in the world. How many years had Rebecca spent thinking her father didn't care about them? How many years had she spent thinking the Suttons no longer mattered?

"I told her Mom would be proud," Bethany agreed.

"She'd be proud of both of you," Victor said. "During my time on Nantucket, I knew the Veterans' Dinner was important to the community. But tonight, what your grandfather and mother built here really hit home." He paused, then added, "We have to fight to save the Sutton Book Club. We have to do whatever it takes. For your mother's sake. And for your grandfather's memory."

Bethany and Rebecca were quiet. The intensity of Victor's words frightened them. Rebecca nodded slowly, although she had no idea how they would save the Sutton Book Club. She didn't have over one hundred thousand dollars just lying around.

"Let's have a glass of wine before we start cleaning," Bethany suggested after a moment of silence.

"Agreed," Rebecca said.

As Bethany poured glasses, Rebecca set up the Bluetooth speaker to play soft music. Outside, night had fallen, and the temperature had dropped, shrouding the old colonial with a chill. Rebecca donned an old Nantucket sweatshirt and raised her wineglass to her father and sister. "To a successful night."

"One to remember," Bethany agreed.

For a little while, they could pretend everything was okay. They chatted gently about easy memories they'd shared together, about the sailboat they'd once had, and about the puppy they'd adopted, who'd died not long after Victor had left. All the while, Esme seemed like a ghost hovering around them. Valerie seemed even further away —an entity none of them knew anything about.

"Have either of you heard from your little sister?" Victor asked, his eyes far away. He sensed the missing pieces of their family, as well.

Rebecca and Bethany shook their heads.

"On Facebook, it says she lives in Seattle," Rebecca explained. "But we don't know if it's up to date."

"Seattle." Victor said the city's name as though it were a foreign language. "A few years back, I read about an event she planned. It was worth millions of dollars."

"Yeah. Valerie was in and out of the news for a while. She rubbed shoulders with celebrities and even dated a few of them," Bethany affirmed. "It always made me nervous when she suddenly dropped off the face of the news sites. As one of her big sisters, it was devastating that I couldn't keep track of her. And then, even the news couldn't tell me where she was or who she was with."

"No news felt so much worse," Rebecca agreed.

"Isn't it strange that we were just in our separate cities, googling each other?" Bethany asked quietly.

"We should have picked up the phone," Victor whispered. "No, correction. I should have picked up the phone."

Rebecca's stomach was in knots. She'd never envisioned this reunion, and now that it was happening, she wasn't sure what to make of it.

"Dad?" Bethany began tentatively.

Victor raised his eyebrows.

"What is going on with you?" she stuttered. "I mean, I know you're getting divorced. And I'm sorry about that. I really am." She paused and shook her head, surprised she'd even said it. "But you're a pretty famous psychologist. You've appeared on talk shows and helped prestigious families through difficult times. Didn't the president mention you recently as an example of good mental health? And you've written, what, ten books that give life advice?"

Victor sucked in his cheeks. Even to Rebecca, every single one of Bethany's words seemed like an attack.

"Don't you have meetings? Clients to see? Talk shows to appear on? Book signings to go to?" Bethany demanded. "How can you just be here, in Nantucket, chasing after your ex-wife? How can you be here with us, with nowhere else to be?"

The same questions had plagued Rebecca. The two Sutton sisters watched Victor as he contemplated how to answer. All the color drained from his cheeks. It was clear his answers were not easy ones.

But just as Victor opened his lips to speak, the front door screamed open. *Who could be here at this hour?*

Hadn't all the veterans left already? Rebecca leaped to her feet to inspect, just as familiar voices began to echo.

"I just can't understand it. I can't." An older woman's voice was overwhelmed with exhaustion.

"Mom. Hold my arm." It was a younger woman's voice, exasperated and slightly frightened.

"I'm holding it." The older woman groaned. "Why would they do this? What has gotten into them?"

"Come on, Mom."

Bethany and Rebecca locked eyes. Next came the sound of footsteps making their way closer. Someone gasped for breath. Across the table, Victor placed his face in his hands as his shoulders shook. It was as though a monster from the past came into view and wanted to swallow them hole.

It could only be Esme Gardner and Valerie Sutton. They were seconds from being all together again. And the intensity was almost too much to bear.

Chapter Sixteen

Rebecca, Bethany, and Victor stood frozen as Valerie and Esme appeared. Rebecca's heart beat so frantically that she could hardly hear anything else. When they reached the second story, Valerie and Esme paused, arms linked, and looked at the rest of the Suttons with panicked eyes. It was a face-off.

"Mom..." Rebecca breathed. She took a tentative step forward but held herself back. The sight of her mother, so many years after they'd last hugged one another, so many years after they'd last spoken, was remarkably painful.

Just as it had to all of them, time had aged Esme. Her hair was a silvery white, and her body seemed smaller and frail. She wore a black dress that hugged her tiny figure, and her blue eyes shone with a mix of curiosity and fear. In every respect, she was beautiful, with high cheekbones, a regal lift to her chin, and long fingers. She looked like a painting.

Beside her, Valerie was a beauty in her late thirties. Just like Bethany and Rebecca, she wore her brunette locks long, and although she looked tired and guarded, something about her was stunning.

During these moments of silence, Rebecca was awash with guilt. *How could she have let these people become strangers?*

Before she could think of something to say—something to make sense of any of this, Esme found her voice.

"How dare you?" Esme's lower lip trembled. She dropped her arm from Valerie's and stepped toward them. She looked on the brink of screaming.

Rebecca was caught off guard. She glanced at Bethany, praying Bethany would find a way to get through this. Esme's eyes were strange, far away.

"Mom." Valerie stepped alongside Esme and took her arm again. "We should really get you back home."

Esme shook her head. "My father founded the Sutton Book Club years and years ago. He did it as a selfless act in support of his community. He did it because he cared about Nantucket, about his legacy. And you three dare to storm in here? Stomp all over that legacy?"

Rebecca blinked back tears. She wanted to protest, to tell Esme that they'd all wanted to uphold her grandfather's legacy.

"All I wanted for you was the best," Esme continued, speaking directly to Bethany and Rebecca. She eyed Valerie suspiciously, adding, "I wanted it for you, too."

Anger and fear filled her face. Rebecca blinked back tears.

"Mom? Will you sit down? Please?" Valerie begged.

But suddenly, Esme turned to face Victor, who stood with slumped shoulders. He looked like he wanted to run away from her as fast as he could.

"And you!" Esme cried in a high-pitched and strange

voice. "You! Victor Sutton..." She trailed off, searching for words.

Victor took a small step toward her. Despite the intensity of the silence, he found a way to speak.

All he said was, "I know, Esme. I know."

And just like that, Esme staggered to her knees. The sound was horrendous. She howled with pain. Valerie, Rebecca, and Bethany hurried around her and helped her back to her feet. Tears came torrentially from her eyes. In a moment, they spread her across the floral couch next to the collection of Shakespearean plays. She peered up at the ceiling and whimpered.

"He needs to go," Esme told the ceiling. "Please. Make him go away."

Rebecca turned back toward her father, who had already gathered his things. He bowed his head as he hurried out of sight.

"He's gone, Mom. He's gone," Rebecca murmured.

By the time she turned back, Esme's eyes were closed. She'd fallen into a strange, fitful sleep. Rebecca couldn't breathe. Bethany backed up and fell into one of the dinner chairs, staring at Esme as though she were a ghost. Only Valerie seemed more or less composed.

When Rebecca was sure her mother was fast asleep, she said, "Valerie? Can you tell me what the heck is going on?" She hated how stressed she sounded.

Valerie's eyes flashed. She seemed to have very little respect or love to give.

"I should ask you the same thing," Valerie shot back.

"Is Mom okay?" Bethany asked softly.

Valerie rubbed her temples. "I think so. I don't know."

"Should we call someone?" Rebecca demanded. "Bethany, you're a doctor. What do you think?"

Bethany shook her head. She looked confused.

"We had a long trip." Valerie seemed too exhausted to fight. She staggered back and sat on a chair across from Bethany. Without another word, she poured herself a stiff glass of wine and knocked her head back to drink.

Bethany and Rebecca had a wordless conversation. Bethany lifted one shoulder as a way to say, *Come on. Sit down.* Rebecca inched toward the table, sat, and watched as Bethany poured them both glasses of wine.

Here they sat. The three Sutton sisters. Back together after all this time.

And none of them seemed pleased to see each other.

"You were with Mom all this time?" Rebecca asked. She was careful not to make her tone too sharp.

"All what time?" Valerie asked.

Rebecca counted the days on her fingers. "I've been on the island since the day she left."

Valerie shrugged. "She flew to me. Yeah."

"To Seattle?" Bethany asked.

Valerie arched one of her eyebrows quizzically. "I haven't lived in Seattle for years."

Rebecca and Bethany were quiet, stewing in shame.

After a period of silence, Valerie explained, "I'm in San Francisco now. I moved there for a job."

"Wow," Rebecca said because she wasn't sure what else to say. She turned back to watch the rise and fall of Esme's chest.

"Why did she come out to see you?" Bethany asked.

Valerie looked uncertain if she wanted to continue. "I don't know if you ever knew my high school boyfriend, Zach. We broke up after I left the island, and he stayed here, got married, and had kids. Anyway, I hear from him from time to time. It always makes me so nostalgic for the island."

Rebecca furrowed her brow. She'd left the island before Valerie ever had a boyfriend named Zach. *How much of Valerie's life had she missed?*

"Zach reached out to ask if I'd heard about Larry," Valerie continued. "Although I'd only met him a few times, I couldn't believe he'd died. And so suddenly! I called Mom for the first time in years. I could already tell on the phone that she wasn't herself. Something was off about her." Valerie gestured toward Esme on the couch, who had certainly not seemed mentally well moments before.

"I bought her a ticket to come out to San Francisco with me. I thought we could live there together for a while. The first day or so was tough. She cried a lot and often didn't make sense. I had to take some time off work, which my employers were not pleased with. But I figured, you know, she was one of the only people in my life for a long time. It was my turn to be with her."

Bethany and Rebecca exchanged glances. *Was Valerie using their mother as an excuse for having lost another job?* There was no way to know.

Valerie went on. "But then, Mom started hearing from people back here in Nantucket. She heard that her daughter and ex-husband were hanging around the house, waiting for her? Causing trouble? Asking the police where she was? At first, I didn't want to believe it. It didn't make any sense. I didn't know why either of you would be with Dad—the guy who left us in a lurch after our family's greatest tragedy? But whatever."

Rebecca stuttered. She wanted to explain herself.

"I did my best to keep Mom away from her phone, but it wasn't easy. She's a grown woman grieving. She has to have a way to call her friends. Unfortunately, her friends operated as hourly gossip columnists. Mom got more and more anxious. I tried to calm her down, to tell her she needed to focus on herself right now and not whatever baloney was happening on Nantucket. But then she started getting emails about another godforsaken Veterans' Dinner. That reminded her of the stupid Book Club, and her father, and everything she'd ever promised him. So now, we're here. And she's exhausted and depressed and almost out of her mind."

Valerie was livid. Rebecca felt like a kid in the principal's office. Bethany's cheeks were pink.

"Valerie..." Rebecca breathed. "We tried to call you."

Valerie rolled her eyes. "I don't think you have my number."

"The one listed on Facebook?" Rebecca asked.

Valerie shook her head. "That hasn't been my number for years."

"But you could have reached out to us," Rebecca insisted. "Especially when you heard that Dad and I were on Nantucket. I was worried sick when Mom was missing."

"She was never missing," Valerie shot back. "I was taking care of her."

"Dad and I came here because we wanted to make sure she was okay, too!" Rebecca quaked with anger and sorrow.

"Yeah. That brings me to the most pressing issue of all," Valerie sputtered. "Can you explain why you thought coming here with him was a good idea?"

Rebecca blinked at her little sister. *How could she*

possibly translate the size of her own grief? "He came to Maine. He... he told me Mom wasn't doing well. He told me he wasn't doing well, either."

"Oh. Boo-hoo." Valerie's nostrils flared. "Victor Sutton had a bad day, and you ran to the rescue? Is that what I'm hearing?"

Rebecca bent her head. Bethany placed her hand on Rebecca's shoulder. For a long time, the three Sutton sisters were very quiet.

"Did Mom tell you she's about to lose the Sutton Book Club?" Rebecca asked the floor.

Valerie made a small noise. "What?"

Confusion made the air taut.

"I found some mail back at the house," Rebecca continued. "The timing couldn't be worse."

"She owes money?" Valerie demanded.

"Much more than I have," Rebecca said with a shrug.

"There's no way we can explain everything," Bethany said. "Not here. Not with Mom so sick."

Valerie nodded and stood. Rebecca watched as she walked around the table and stood over their mother. With a tender hand, she brushed their mother's hair back. As far as Rebecca knew, Valerie never had any children— but her motherly instincts were clear.

"Mom?" Valerie's voice was very sweet.

Esme stirred on the couch and rubbed her eyes. Valerie called her name a few more times until Esme's eyes slowly opened. She searched the room to discover all three of her daughters, and her face twitched with confusion.

"Valerie, I have a terrible headache," she said meekly.

"Let's go home," Valerie said. She dropped onto the

couch, laced her arm over Esme's shoulders, and helped her to her feet.

With a sudden burst of energy, Rebecca and Bethany rose from their chairs. Rebecca held the other side of Esme as Bethany bustled behind them, grabbing jackets and purses. They wordlessly decided to come back to the Sutton Book Club tomorrow to tend to the dishes. Tonight was the night for family drama.

With Esme safe in the car she and Valerie had come in, Rebecca and Bethany drove back to the old Victorian in the SUV. Mostly, they were quiet. A few times, when the emotions were too powerful, they spoke. Rebecca said, "I can't believe this is happening," and Bethany said, "Mom doesn't look very good." Rebecca added, "I hope Dad doesn't disappear on us now." But Bethany didn't respond to that.

In the driveway, Rebecca turned off the engine and watched as Valerie helped their mother through the front door. From a distance, Esme looked like a feeble old woman.

"Let's go help her," Rebecca whispered.

Rebecca and Bethany hurried from the SUV, through the front door, and up the staircase. Already, Esme and Valerie crept toward the bedroom Esme had once shared with Victor so many years ago. It was the largest of the upstairs bedrooms, with an immaculate view of the Nantucket Sound and the wide stretch of beach that so often glowed with impossible beauty. Just now, it was dark, and nothing but a void of black could be seen out the window.

Rebecca and Bethany stopped in the doorway of the bedroom. Esme sat on the edge of the bed as Valerie hurried around her, grabbing a nightgown from the closet, some night cream, and a thick pair of socks. It occurred to Rebecca that her mother became cold at night due to her age. Valerie had clearly learned this during their time in San Francisco.

"Do you want to brush your teeth before you go to sleep, Mom?" Valerie asked sweetly.

Rebecca's throat was tight. All she wanted in the world was to throw herself into that room and help her sister tend to her mother. All she wanted was to show how much she cared.

But there wasn't much to do. Valerie had Esme tucked beneath the cloud-like comforter in just a few minutes. Valerie stepped lightly toward Bethany and Rebecca and pressed her finger to her lips.

"She's already asleep," she whispered.

Once in the hallway, Valerie closed the door quietly. The three Sutton sisters stood in the shadows of the house they'd grown up in and regarded one another.

"Is Dad in the guest room?" Rebecca asked.

Valerie shrugged. She eyed the closed doors of the hallway, behind which were each of their former bedrooms. "It's eerie being up here," she muttered. "I visited Mom a few times over the years, but I never found a reason to come upstairs."

Valerie stepped toward the door that had once been hers, turned the knob, and opened the door. With her face in the doorway, Rebecca could just make out bits and pieces from Valerie's youth. Slowly, Valerie stepped back and turned to show the ghastly glow of her face.

"It's almost the same," she said. "Yours, too?"

Rebecca and Bethany nodded. They'd gone through this all before.

Valerie grimaced and shut the door to her bedroom.

And then, with her face resolute, she turned on her heel and marched toward the one door Rebecca hadn't dared to open. Only Victor had tried it on their first day, and Rebecca had slammed it shut.

Valerie heaved a sigh in front of that door. Rebecca wanted to cry out, to tell her not to open it. But, beyond anything, she knew it had to be Valerie who opened it. She had the right.

The door creaked open, and Valerie stepped through as though it was just another day. Rebecca watched from several feet back. Valerie's feet were soft on the old carpeting as her fingers traced the old blue comforter on the bed. The desk under the window contained awards from childhood—tiny statues and plaques that ensured children understood that hard work was meaningful. Numerous paintings and drawings hung on the walls as proof of tremendous creativity.

Rebecca was unable to breathe. Beside her, Bethany had both hands over her mouth as though she was afraid she would cry out.

Valerie stood in the center of that room and turned back to face them. Her chin wiggled with sorrow, and her eyes filled with tears. When she fell back onto the bed, Bethany and Rebecca did the impossible, too. They crossed the doorway's threshold, sat on either side of Valerie, and wrapped their arms around her. They joined her in crying for the brother they'd lost so many years ago.

Losing Joel still felt like yesterday. And none of them had ever really gotten over it.

Chapter Seventeen

1992

Joel Sutton loved baseball. At nine years old, he was the fastest in his baseball league, whipping around the bases at lightning speed as the white ball soared through a blue June sky. His family cheered for him in the stands and yelled out his name. "You can make it, Joel! Come on!" They were the Sutton family, one of the kindest and openhearted families on the island of Nantucket. Wherever they went and whatever they did, they were together.

Rebecca was the eldest of the Sutton children. At fourteen, she was five years older than Joel and not always so keen on sitting around a baseball game on a Saturday when she could have been with her friends at the beach. Then again, she was one of the loudest in the stands, jumping up and down with her sisters, Bethany and Valerie, as Joel stampeded to home base. This home run meant his team won. It meant they could all finally leave the baseball fields and take their father's new sailboat for a spin.

Rebecca and Bethany hustled down the stands to grab the fence that wrapped around the baseball field. "Joel! You did it!" Rebecca cried, and Bethany echoed it. At twelve, Bethany was eager to be everything Rebecca was, so much so that she copied almost everything Rebecca did. This annoyed Rebecca to no end. In fact, it was one of the main reasons for any yelling in the Sutton home.

Valerie, their ten-year-old sister, rushed up behind them. To Bethany and Rebecca, Valerie seemed like just a little kid. Her legs were a little too long for her body, and her hair was wild and unbrushed. To them, she would never keep up with her older sisters.

Joel jogged around the baseball fence and high-fived Bethany and Rebecca, clearly pleased with himself. He only hugged Valerie. The two of them jumped up and down joyously as Valerie's chaotic hair glistened in the sunlight.

"There they are. The Sutton twins." Mrs. Walton, their next-door neighbor, stepped up to say hello.

Valerie and Joel laughed. Valerie had on Joel's baseball hat, and her freckles stood out across her nose and cheeks. It was true what Mrs. Walton said. Since forever, Valerie and Joel had been inseparable. They were just one year apart and fascinated with most of the same stuff —bugs, sports, being outside, reading, and playing pranks on their older sisters. They even seemed to have a secret language all their own. Rebecca had noticed—it was as though they could read one another's minds.

Their mother, Esme Sutton, made her way down the stands, adjusting her baseball hat before she dropped down to wrap her arms around Joel. She was unafraid of dirt and sweat and preferred to be the mother who liked messes. "Messes aren't permanent," she always used to say.

"You were great, Joel!" Esme cried.

Their father, the tall and powerful Victor Sutton, appeared beside Esme and put his arm around her. Together, the parents beamed down at their children, so sure of their love. Rebecca had never gone a day without feeling protected and at peace.

"Are you kids ready for the sailing adventure of your lives?" Victor asked.

"Yeah!" the four of them cried, pumping their fists in the air.

"Joel! You're bleeding again." Valerie pointed at Joel's face, where a line of red hung from his nostrils. Suddenly, the line became a river, coating his lips and chin.

"Oh dear." Esme rifled through her purse for a package of tissues, which she always had on her for these occasions. Joel's nosebleeds had become as commonplace as rainstorms and tourist traffic. "Lift your chin and press your nostrils together, buddy. Just like always."

Joel did as he was told but still chatted excitedly with Valerie, who'd just read a story about a newly discovered bug. Victor spoke gently to Esme, whispering in her ear lovingly. Together, Bethany and Rebecca leaned against the fence, pretending to be too cool for school. Up at the top of the stands sat Tommy Tucker, the biggest crush of Rebecca's life. Bethany dug her elbow into Rebecca's upper arm.

"Ow!" Rebecca cried.

"Don't you see who's at the top of the bleachers?" Bethany asked.

"Of course, I do! But you can't just point at people,"

Rebecca muttered. In a whisper, she added, "You have to be cool, Bethany."

Bethany took the information and nodded. Of all the Sutton children, she was the most hyper-intelligent, which pleased Victor. Although Rebecca was two years older than Bethany, Bethany could already do complicated mathematics equations. She talked about becoming a doctor or a scientist someday.

"I think it's clearing up," Joel announced as he removed the tissue from his nose and inspected it.

"Oh, good. You must be dehydrated." Esme pressed a bottle of water into his hands and smiled at him. "Drink all of this, okay?"

Joel told her he would.

The four kids and two adults set out for the harbor, where Victor had tied up his new sailboat. Joel swung his baseball mitt at his side as he sang a song with Valerie. Rebecca walked slightly behind Esme and Victor, who spoke in the low tones of adults who didn't want to be overheard.

"Did the doctor call back yet?" Victor asked Esme.

"He said we need to go to a specialist," Esme returned. "But it doesn't make sense. I mean, he's a healthy kid. Didn't you just see him make that home run?"

"I'm sure it's nothing serious," Victor affirmed. "But if we have to go to Boston, we have to go to Boston. I can take a few days off work this week."

Esme squeezed his upper arm. "That's sweet of you. You're so good to us."

Victor stopped briefly and adjusted a curl behind her ear. The look in his eyes told Rebecca everything she needed to know about love. It was real—and it was significant.

Would she and Tommy Tucker ever feel that way about each other? Was it possible she would ever find love?

Victor's sailboat was a beautiful vessel with the name *ESME* written across the side. Bethany and Rebecca rolled their eyes at their father's cheesiness as Valerie and Joel hopped on and marveled at the ropes and the sails. Since they were children, they'd frequently sailed on their father's old boat, which hadn't fit them all comfortably.

As Rebecca was the oldest of the Sutton children, she was in charge of operating some of the ropes. She tied intricate sailor's knots—the bowline, the reef knot, and the clove hitch. Bethany was still trying to get the hang of the bowline. As the sails burst open and the boat glided in the open water, Valerie and Joel clung to the side railings and screamed at the water below. Their joy was youthful and electric. At fourteen, Rebecca already understood that you couldn't get back your youth once you'd lost it.

For a little while, Victor sailed the family around the island. The beauty of their home intoxicated the Suttons. When they saw their Victorian on the shoreline, they called and waved to it, praying their dog would run outside to say hello to them. Their love lived in that home. They were safe and happy in that home. They ate meals and told stories and got a little bit older every single day in that home.

* * *

The week after that sailing adventure, Joel and Victor visited Boston to see a specialist about Joel's nosebleeds. Until that time, nobody had mentioned the word "cancer" yet. That happened to other people. Not the Suttons.

The Saturday after the appointment with the specialist, Rebecca wanted to go to a birthday party. A girl in her class had invited her, and she was pretty sure Tommy Tucker would be there. Bethany begged to go with Rebecca, and Rebecca spent the morning telling her it was only for "older" kids over thirteen.

But around noon, Esme knocked on Rebecca's bedroom door and beckoned Bethany and Rebecca to the living room for a family meeting. Esme's eyes contained dark circles beneath them. Rebecca was suddenly frightened about her mother and how much she'd seemed to age in only a few days. *Was that how aging happened? Did it happen all at once?*

Downstairs, Victor sat in his cushioned reading chair. He bent over his knees with eyes similar to Esme's. Rebecca and Bethany sat across from him on the couch as their mother stood.

"Where's Valerie?" Rebecca asked.

But at that moment, Valerie burst down the stairs. Her hair was wild and unkempt, and she had paint on her fingers. She sat between Bethany and Rebecca and bounced on the couch cushion.

"Where's Joel?" Valerie asked.

Esme and Victor eyed one another. Rebecca's stomach was in knots.

"Your brother is in his bedroom sleeping," Esme replied.

"Do you want us to wake him up for the family meeting?" Bethany asked.

Esme shook her head. "He needs his rest right now." She looked on the verge of falling over.

Victor clasped and unclasped his hands. "Your brother has been diagnosed with leukemia. Do you know what that is?"

Bethany shot up from the couch, her face stricken. As their mini-scientist, she knew about many types of diseases. "You can't be serious," she said.

Beside Rebecca, Valerie was very stiff. She glanced at her face, which seemed hollow and strange.

Victor went on to explain that leukemia was a type of cancer in the bone marrow and blood. Soon, Joel would begin chemotherapy, which would attack both the cancer and Joel's healthy cells at once. This didn't make sense to Rebecca. *Why would Joel's medicine hurt Joel?* Still, she didn't want to sound stupid. She had to be the brave older sister.

"How can we help?" Bethany asked, sounding more confident and sure of herself than Rebecca felt.

"Well, it's difficult to say right now," Victor began.

"We need to be strong for your brother," Esme continued. "He'll need our love and support more now than ever."

"But we're the Suttons," Victor continued. "We're the strongest family I know. We can fight this together."

"Joel isn't alone," Esme said. "He knows we're here for him. He knows we'll get through this."

On the couch, Valerie clutched both Rebecca's and Bethany's knees. The look in her eyes was sharp and bizarre. Like Valerie, Rebecca wasn't sure she believed what her parents said. *How could Esme and Victor have any say in what cancer could or couldn't do? How could their love fight cancer?*

But then again, Esme and Victor were their parents. The Sutton sisters had to trust them.

Later, Joel woke up and walked downstairs in his socks and pajamas to eat soup and grilled cheese sandwiches with his sisters. They sat on the back porch and listened to the seagulls cawing overhead. Together, he and Valerie gabbed about a type of shark they both liked as Rebecca studied her brother's face. *He looked just the same as ever. How could he be so sick?*

Rebecca was five when her parents had baby Joel. She'd taken on whatever responsibilities she could, which had intensified as she turned six, seven, and eight. Sometimes, she felt her love for Valerie and Joel was different than her love for Bethany since she remembered when they were so helpless. She remembered how much they'd needed her.

"There they are. My favorite kids in the world." Victor stepped out of the house to join them on the porch, wearing a strained smile.

Esme remained in the kitchen, cleaning a skillet with a sponge. She seemed to scrub it forever, long after any bit of grease had dripped off. Rebecca watched her through the window, mesmerized. For the first time, she realized her mother didn't have control over everything. The world did not go out of its way for your happiness. It was the first time she was really afraid.

Chapter Eighteen

Present Day

Careful not to touch anything in Joel's bedroom, they sat at the edge of the bed and took in the sight of his shirts in the closet, his baseball shoes next to the dresser, and the art their mother had hung on the walls. In some ways, Joel could have walked through the door at any moment, leaped on the bed, and demanded that one of his older sisters play with him.

"It's been so long since he passed," Rebecca breathed.

Bethany held both of her elbows nervously. Valerie looked listless. It was as though the energy in the room ate them alive. Rebecca stood and walked toward the hallway. She wanted to drag her sisters out of there and tell them they couldn't fall so deeply into the past. As though they sensed it too, they soon followed after her. Valerie shut the door slowly and spread her palm over it as though she could feel the room's heartbeat. Then she repeated what Rebecca had thought on the very first day. "It's a museum."

Downstairs, Bethany grabbed a bottle of wine from the cabinet and poured each of the sisters a glass. They sat at the breakfast table and drank silently. Another storm brewed outside, and the windows rattled in their panes.

"One of the first things Dad did when we got here was open that door," Rebecca whispered. "I couldn't believe it. I slammed it in his face immediately."

"I would have done the same thing," Bethany agreed.

Valerie chewed the inside of her cheek. She looked contemplative. "How old were Mom and Dad when Joel died?"

It had never occurred to Rebecca to consider this. "Joel died when he was ten," she began. "I was fifteen."

"I was thirteen," Bethany said.

"And I was eleven," Valerie added. These ages were crystal in their minds, as they were the ages when everything in their lives had completely fallen apart.

"Dad's seventy," Rebecca calculated, "which means he was forty when Joel died."

"And Mom was thirty-nine," Valerie whispered.

"They were younger than we are today." Bethany pointed out what was on everyone's mind. "My gosh. To me, they were these impossibly strong and powerful people. It made no sense when they started to fall apart."

"Yet..." Rebecca trailed off for a moment. She was filled with compassion. Finally, she locked eyes with Valerie and said, "My husband died in January. It was a terrible car accident, and it completely blindsided the kids and me."

Valerie's jaw dropped. "Oh, Rebecca. I'm so sorry." The silence stretched between them. "You should have called me."

Rebecca couldn't begin to tell Valerie just how unlikely that would have been. "His death was so debilitating. I struggled to keep going. Even now, almost six months after the accident, I find myself reeling. But more than that, it was remarkable how much I thought about Joel. Joel's death was my very first understanding of it. He had been this bright, confident, and alive little boy. And then suddenly, he was exhausted and so skinny and so, so sick."

Valerie's cheeks drained of color. "I don't like remembering him that way."

"Me neither," Rebecca sputtered. "But Fred's death made me understand just how little we dealt with Joel's death."

"And Dad was a child psychologist!" Valerie cried angrily. "He should have been able to help us."

But Rebecca was no longer so sure about that. She palmed the back of her neck and considered how irresponsible she'd been in the weeks and months after Fred's death. "I think for Dad, the world ended with Joel's death. He could no longer make sense of anything, least of all his career."

"He certainly went off and made something of himself," Valerie scoffed. "With Bree."

"There's no forgiving what Dad did," Bethany tried. "But now that I'm married, I understand that every marriage operates with its own set of rules. Mom and Dad loved each other. They did."

Rebecca nodded, remembering.

"But after being thrown into hell, they just couldn't find a way to come back together again," Bethany continued.

Valerie looked defeated. "I know. I haven't been married. So you're saying I couldn't understand?"

"No!" Bethany cried.

"That's not it at all," Rebecca fumbled. "I think what Bethany is trying to say is..." She trailed off, searching for the right words. "I'm forty-five right now, but I still feel young and naive almost every single day. Nobody gave me a how-to manual for losing the love of my life. Nobody gave me a how-to manual about losing my baby brother. And nobody gave me a how-to manual about cleaning up any of the mess we've created over the years. Maybe it's a surprise to you that I even want to clean this up. Trust me. It's a surprise to me, too."

Valerie's eyes were difficult to read. *Being forty-one and having made so many public mistakes, couldn't she understand that being an adult was no easy feat?*

Finally, after a long, pregnant pause, Valerie spoke. "Remember how after Joel died, we never spoke of him?"

Rebecca and Bethany nodded, their gaze on the table with shame.

"The way I remember it, this big house was so drafty and empty after Joel's death," Valerie continued. "You both were always off with friends. Apparently, Dad was off with Bree. And Mom? I don't even know where Mom was. Probably, she was at that stupid Sutton Book Club."

Rebecca bristled. Valerie was hard-edged and still filled with pain.

"Nobody is saying any of that is okay," Rebecca said.

Valerie sniffed. Her eyes were lost. "I can't promise you I'll stay much longer. I just want to make sure Mom is set up. I want to get her into therapy, but I don't want to deal with Dad. We were all a mess after Joel died. All of us! But we were his mess, and he left us here. I don't know how either of you can ever forgive him for that."

* * *

The storm raged all night and into the morning. As Rebecca dressed in leggings and a big Bar Harbor sweatshirt, gray light shimmered across the bedsheets, and rain flattened against the windowpane.

It was only six, but Rebecca couldn't sleep another wink. Valerie's words had kept her awake all night, and guilt made her stomach ache. At eleven, Valerie hadn't been old enough to take care of herself. Her best friend, Joel, had left the world. Valerie and Bethany had taken refuge in friends, in the community, but Valerie had just gotten harder and built up walls. *Was this why she'd never allowed herself to fall in love and get married? Was this why she'd never had children?*

Rebecca didn't think all women without children were somehow "wrong" or "bad." She had plenty of female friends who'd chosen the no-kids route. None of them had felt abandoned as a child, though. None of them had the stormy eyes of Valerie Sutton.

Rebecca entered the softness of the hallway. A few doors down, Esme's door was cracked, and a female voice murmured. Rebecca went toward it like a moth to the flame. When she knocked on the door, it opened a bit more to reveal Valerie sitting cross-legged in bed next to Esme, who smiled sweetly at her youngest daughter. The sight was enough to break Rebecca's heart.

"Hi, you two," Rebecca said.

Valerie looked tired, as though she'd struggled with

sleep just as much as Rebecca. Thunder roared above the house, and Esme's smile widened.

"When you kids were frightened of the storm, you used to pile into bed with your father and me. All four of you!" Esme shook her head and gazed at the ceiling, lost in the memory. "Of course, it broke my heart when Rebecca and Bethany decided they were too old to seek refuge here."

"Apparently, I'm still not too old," Valerie tried.

Esme beckoned for Rebecca, who walked slowly toward the bed and eventually shimmied under the covers next to Valerie. Her heartbeat felt very slow. Lightning flashed outside the window, and Esme said she was sorry for all the tourists who'd come to the island that June. "We've gotten so much rain."

Rebecca was grateful to see her mother so soft and docile after her stress the previous night. She chatted gently about her flower and vegetable gardens, and about how sorry she was that Larry couldn't see how big the tomatoes had already grown.

"Larry always ate his tomatoes raw with salt and pepper," Esme continued. Her eyes were thoughtful. "Your father never would have had that. He preferred all of his vegetables cooked."

For the first time, Rebecca realized that Larry's death had probably had the same effect on Esme as Fred's had on her. It had dragged the horrors of Joel's death to the surface. It had compounded their grieving.

Another lightning and an immediate clap of thunder filled the sky. Footfalls came down the hallway, followed by Bethany's sweet face in the doorway. Her eyes widened at the sight of her two sisters and mother in bed together.

"Bethy! Oh, Bethy. Come here." Esme lifted her ballerina's hand from beneath the comforter and waved her in.

Bethany hesitated. She probably sensed how emotional this was for all of them. *Could she trust it?* But as another gust of wind rushed against the house, she tiptoed across the room and whipped under the covers. She cuddled next to Rebecca, her cold feet momentarily chilling Rebecca's toes.

"My three daughters. Lucky me," Esme breathed.

For a moment, everyone was quiet, listening to the storm. On the first floor, Victor was alone in his bedroom, probably watching the waves twist and shake across the beach. What he'd done all those years ago kept him apart. He knew it, and the Sutton women knew it.

But what did it mean that he'd come all the way back?

"Rebecca?" Esme's voice was very sweet.

"What is it, Mom?" It took Rebecca everything not to burst into tears.

"Thank you for having the Veterans' Dinner last night," Esme continued. "I was angry. So angry that you took the reins on the Sutton Book Club, but when I woke up this morning, I had so many emails from the veterans complimenting you and the Book Club and the dinner. I'm not sure we can ever go back to the old ways. I'm not a professional chef, as you know. Maybe they'll kick me to the curb." She laughed kindly.

Rebecca propped herself up on her hand and studied her mother's face, which glowed from various face creams and the soft gray light outside. "The veteran community respects and loves you so much, Mom. They need those dinners more than I understood. I'm sorry I went behind your back to host one. I just..." She trailed off. "I wanted to prove to you how much I respect what you're doing at the Book Club. I wanted to show you that so much of my heart apparently still lives here... in Nantucket. And I never could have guessed that, not after so many years away."

Esme shifted her head slightly to lock eyes with Rebecca. "What your grandfather started there is very important to me. I still miss him so much, but it's a way to carry his memory forward."

Rebecca thought of Joel's bedroom and the fact that they never spoke of him after his death. Still, his name was too painful to say in front of Esme just now as they cuddled close together in a single bed as the winds and rain had their way with them.

Suddenly, the phone on the bedside table began to ring. Esme leaped toward it and squinted to read the name on the screen. A moment later, she answered, "Doug? Are you all right?"

Rebecca's heartbeat quickened.

"Oh. Oh, dear me. Doug, I'm so sorry to hear that." Esme twisted so that her feet hung over the side of the bed. "Goodness. Do you need help?"

Rebecca, Bethany, and Valerie all shifted up to press their backs against the headboard. None of them knew what to do. It was as though they'd just woken up to remember they were in their forties.

Very soon, Esme got off the phone. "That's just terrible," she whispered as she placed the phone on the bedside table.

"What happened?" Rebecca asked.

"Doug's old house is a disaster," Esme said. "The recent storms have really taken a toll on it. Apparently, a big tree limb crashed through the window in the living room. Doug's been sleeping in there since he has a massive hole in the ceiling of his bedroom."

Rebecca jumped from the bed, suddenly anxious. All she could think of was Ben, who cared for Doug in that ancient, broken-down house all by himself. "I'm going to go check on them," she said firmly.

"Oh. Would you?" Esme asked.

"Can you give me directions to their house?"

"Of course." Esme described the route to Rebecca, explaining that Doug and Ben lived in a once-beautiful home along the coast. "It would probably cost millions to live there now, but Doug's been on the island forever. He got the property from his parents, who got it from theirs."

Rebecca thanked her mother. "You three will be in contact?" she asked her sisters and mother, who remained in bed.

"We'll be here all morning long," Bethany said. "Go. Make sure they're all right."

Rebecca nodded. She then hurried to her bedroom, where she dressed in jeans, a T-shirt, and a spring jacket. Downstairs, she found her father sitting in the shadows of the living room with a thick book on his lap. He looked listless.

She was surprised to see him there. *Had he heard the Sutton women upstairs, attempting to heal from the events of the past without him?*

"Dad..." Rebecca began.

Victor startled. After a moment, he managed to smile. "Hi. Good morning." He adjusted in the chair. "Where are you off to?"

Rebecca furrowed her brow. "It's Doug and Ben. A

169

tree limb came through their living room window. I want to go make sure they're all right."

Victor's eyes widened. Just when Rebecca thought the morning couldn't get any stranger, he asked, "Can I go with you?"

And for reasons Rebecca couldn't understand, she said, "Of course. Let's go."

Chapter Nineteen

The damage in the old house couldn't have been worse. Ben stood many feet from the gaping hole with his coffee mug lifted, watching as fresh rain fluttered across Doug's bed. Despite the chill, Ben's T-shirt was soaked with sweat because he'd just hauled the television from the living room and unplugged all electrical devices in the area.

Doug sat wrapped up in his winter coat at the kitchen table in front of an untouched bowl of oatmeal and a mug of coffee. Since the enormous crash forty minutes ago, they'd hardly spoken to one another.

Sounding listless, Doug confessed, "I called Esme."

Ben turned to look at Doug, genuinely surprised. It was a rare thing for Doug to ask for help. The Veterans' Dinners were something else; they were on offer and not requested. This proved just how frightened Doug actually was. All this time, Ben had thought Doug had simply shrugged off the continued destruction of his beautiful family home, but he'd been wrong.

"What did she say?" Ben asked. Feeling chilled, he

removed his T-shirt and put on his winter coat, then sat across from Doug at the table.

"She asked if we needed any help," Doug admitted.

"And what did you say?"

Doug coughed and sipped his coffee. "I told her we'd be fine."

Ben understood what had happened. In a moment of fear, Doug had called the closest living relative to Thomas, whom he'd been at war with. It was Doug's way of crying for help.

Outside, car tires splashed through mud puddles. Ben turned to watch as Rebecca rushed from the driver's side. Her hair was a mess. As she opened the back door of her SUV, her hair flattened to her forehead and cheeks. Her father stepped from the passenger door, his eyes shadowed as he regarded the old house. He'd probably never lived in such a state of squalor. He'd probably had a warm and comfy bed all his life.

Ben couldn't blame a man like that for his good fortune no more than he could blame himself for his lack of luck.

Rebecca pulled cups of coffee and a big cardboard box from the back of the SUV. She handed the coffees to Victor, who rushed through the rain to the front porch. By the time he reached the door, Ben was there to open it.

"Hi there!" Ben's voice cracked. He smiled past Victor to Rebecca, who looked as though she'd slept about as much as he had.

Victor stepped through the front door and assessed the tree limb and the glass that had flashed across the hardwood floors of the old house. "Wow," he breathed.

Rebecca handed Ben the cardboard box. "I'm not sure if you're hungry, but we brought donuts."

Ben thanked her, overwhelmed with appreciation. He knew that sometimes food was the only way people knew to translate how sorry they were. This was probably doubly so with Rebecca since she was a chef.

"I hope you weren't in that bed when the tree came through?" Victor asked Doug.

Doug's shoulders shook with laughter. "You bet your bottom dollar I was. It's nothing I can't handle. Just a little rain and wind."

"And glass. And wood," Rebecca pointed out, furrowing her brow. As time passed, her worry intensified.

Doug waved a hand. "What do you have there? Something besides rabbit food?" He pushed the oatmeal to the side and teased Ben, "You know I don't have long to live, right? Would you want to spend your last days eating oatmeal?"

Ben rolled his eyes and watched as Doug inspected the wide selection of donuts. He selected one with maple icing and smiled to himself. At that moment, Ben could almost imagine his appearance as a little boy— before the war. Before his divorce and his second wife's death. Before his children had left him in Nantucket all alone.

"Do you have a broom?" Rebecca asked Ben. "Let's get to work cleaning this up."

"You don't have to do that," Ben assured her.

But Rebecca gave him a look that said she meant business. Ben knew better than to argue with her. He entered the kitchen, grabbed a broom and a dustpan from the cabinet, and returned to find Victor had left.

"Where's your dad?"

"He had to run out for a minute," Rebecca explained

as she took the broom. Through the window, Ben watched as Victor reversed the SUV onto the street.

Wordlessly, they got to work. Ben picked up the larger pieces of glass with his fingers and set them aside on a big towel. Rebecca swept the smaller shards into the dustbin. Slowly, they worked their way to the big hole in the wall.

By the time they reached the window, Victor had returned with supplies from the nearby hardware store. It seemed he'd purchased half the store—tarps, nails, a drill, fresh wood, and a saw. He stepped between Rebecca and Ben, put on a pair of thick gloves, and shoved the enormous branch away from the house. It fell with a thunk on the damp ground.

Rebecca began to remove the sheets from the damp bed. Ben explained that he'd already moved the bed into the living room because Doug's bedroom upstairs had a massive hole in the ceiling.

"Did you call someone to fix it?" Rebecca asked as she wadded up the sheets.

Ben grimaced and eyed Doug. *How could he describe to this beautiful and successful woman that he and Doug barely had two pennies to rub together? How could he tell her that even the most recent dishwashing job he'd applied for hadn't called him back?* He was washed up. Unwanted. Broke.

"I've been waiting to put together some extra funds," Ben explained.

Rebecca nodded. Her eyes weren't judgmental. Ben wanted to place his head on her shoulder and cry. It had been so long since anyone had assured him that everything would be all right. Maybe that was because everything wouldn't be.

Victor stepped into Doug's bedroom to assess the ceiling. Rebecca and Ben followed him.

"That's quite a hole," Victor said. Although Ben had tried to patch it up with the materials he had around the house, it still dripped from the new storm.

"What's in that box?" Rebecca pointed at an old cardboard box in the corner, upon which Ben had put a number of old pieces of wood and his hammer. Nothing in the house was of any value, so he hadn't thought anything of it.

"Not sure. Doug's old stuff, I guess," Ben said.

Rebecca hurried forward, removed the slabs of wood and the hammer, and took the lid from the box. Her messy hair fell to the side of her face. Ben crossed his arms over his chest and tried not to think about how beautiful she was. As a successful chef from a prestigious family, she was so far out of his league it wasn't even funny. Still, that didn't change the fact that he'd dreamed of her when he'd managed to sleep last night.

"My gosh. These books look old!" Rebecca pointed in the box and turned back, her eyebrows high. She then tugged at the damp box, pulling it across the floor toward a drier area. "Is that German?" Rebecca asked.

Ben had never thought to look inside Doug's secret box of things. But just as Rebecca said, the books within this box were all in German. They were thick and expertly bound and clearly from a long-ago era. Rebecca lifted one of the books from the box and flicked it open to show gorgeous illustrations. The only thing was that the books were waterlogged, and the pages bubbled. Whatever value they would have had was clearly gone.

"Who knows how many times those books have been

rained on," Ben said with a sigh as he peered over Rebecca's shoulder.

"But they're gorgeous," Rebecca whispered. She flipped to the beginning of the book to find the copyright year. "1912. Germany."

Throughout this time, Victor leaned against the bedroom wall, watching them. He said nothing. Ben noted the mysterious look in his eyes but soon shrugged it off and stepped through the living room to find Doug in the kitchen. Rebecca hurried after him with another of the old German books.

"Doug?" Ben held the book up to show the cover. "Did you bring these back from Germany?"

Doug placed a half-eaten donut back on a plate and nodded. His eyes shimmered with memories. "Remember those girls I told you about? Thomas's wife and the two others? Their fathers had enormous collections of beautiful books. We went back to Scherfede a few times for dances and meals and got to know them better. Over candlelight, they did their best to tell us their favorite German fairy tales and stories. They didn't want us to think of them only in terms of the war. They wanted us to think of them as principled men, as intellectuals. And when it was clear we would move to the next camp, they gave us these books to remember them by."

"They're wonderful," Rebecca breathed.

"Yes. I suppose they were," Doug said, eyeing the books with shame. "I haven't been good at taking care of anything over the years. It's a miracle I've survived this long."

"It's still a remarkable story," Rebecca said. "Maybe we can dry them out a little bit so you can enjoy them whenever you want."

Ben and Rebecca returned to Doug's bedroom to retrieve the rest of the books. Victor had returned to the window to sling a big tarp over it. The howling of the wind had already quieted, and the house had begun to warm.

As Rebecca gathered the books in her arms, she locked eyes with Ben. She spoke quietly and kindly. "What about insurance? Is there any way they could help with some of these costs? I mean, this is such a great house. It just needs a bit of care."

Her tone made it clear that the house was minutes from being condemned.

Ben couldn't look at her. "To be honest with you, Doug and I have trouble making ends meet. There's no insurance to speak of." If he were honest, he would have told her he hadn't known Doug to have any insurance since they'd met. "I wish Doug would have told me about these books. Maybe they could have brought in a pretty penny."

"Who knows when they first got wet," Rebecca pointed out. "But they're relics. My mother should be able to help me save them. She was always a master at repairing old books."

The sound of a drill came in the next room, followed by a hammer. Rebecca tilted her head, listening. Very softly, she said, "I haven't seen my father fix anything since I was a little girl. He used to be the master of repairing things. He even built some of our furniture and toys."

"I really appreciate his help," Ben said, although a part of him was ashamed he needed help at all.

Rebecca lifted her eyes. There was a strange tension between them. Ben hated that he couldn't stop thinking of her romantically. Everything else in his life was far too chaotic for anything like that. Besides, the ring glinting on her left finger meant she was married.

"Why don't you come by the Sutton Book Club in a few days? We can break the rules and have two Veterans' Dinners this week," Rebecca said softly. "I love listening to Doug's stories. And I'm sure you and the others have a few stories of your own."

Ben's heart lifted. "You don't have to do that."

"I insist," Rebecca said. "Besides, who knows how much longer my mother will let me cook at the Sutton Book Club? That place is her baby. She rarely lets anyone else take control."

Ben laughed gently. "Doug always says Esme's just about the most stubborn woman in the world. But she got it from her father."

Rebecca's eyes glinted. "I don't think I know anyone who isn't too stubborn for their own good. We should all loosen up every once in a while. We should all admit we're a little bit weaker than we'd like to be if only so we can help one another." She paused, then added, "I think my family would have benefited from that thirty years ago. Now, we're left to pick up the pieces. I just don't know if we'll manage it. But I suppose we have to try."

Chapter Twenty

After Victor set up the tarp to insulate the house, he promised to return tomorrow and the day after that—as many days as it took to ensure the house was livable again. "It'll take some time, but I can get this house into better shape." It was clear he planned to do it for free.

Ben shook his hand and thanked him. "I'll be here to help you. I just never had the tools or the materials to make it happen."

"It's never good to take on a project this big alone. Now that I'm seventy, I guess I'll need the help even more." He tried to smile, but it didn't quite reach his eyes.

"You'll need a place to sleep," Rebecca said, eyeing the damp mattress.

"We have the other one," Ben explained easily. "It dried out from our last incident. Doug will sleep there, and I'll take the couch."

"You're sure?" Rebecca didn't want to push it. Ben seemed anxious from all the attention, as though he wanted to apologize for the destruction of the house. But it wasn't his fault. None of it was. Like all of them, Ben and Doug were victims of their circumstances. All Rebecca and Victor could do was help as much as they could.

In the SUV, Rebecca and Victor were quiet as they drove back to the old Victorian home. Victor stewed in thoughts Rebecca could only guess at as she panicked about Doug and Ben and the Sutton Book Club and all the money in the world that was never available for those who needed it.

Rebecca parked in the driveway and sat in silence for a moment. She wanted her father to say something assuring, but she wasn't sure what. He hadn't been that kind of father since before Joel's diagnosis. Then again, he'd managed to reassure plenty of people as their family psychologist. *Why couldn't he extend that knowledge to his own family?*

Instead, he said, "I won't be staying at the house tonight."

Rebecca cocked her head, surprised. "Why not?"

"It's too much for your mother," he said. "I've asked my brother if I can stay at his place. As you know, we aren't exactly one another's favorite people, either, but he says he has a room for me."

Rebecca nodded. Although she'd strangely gotten used to him over the previous few days, Victor's sudden presence was probably too much for Esme. It certainly enraged Valerie.

"Do you need a ride?" Rebecca asked.

"I can walk," Victor said. He then stepped out onto the driveway, clipped the door closed behind him, waved, and headed toward the street. The rain continued to spit, unwilling to stop. It seemed impossible that summer was around the corner.

Rebecca headed inside and collapsed on the living room couch. She was listless. There was no movement or sound in the rest of the house, and when she checked upstairs, she found Esme asleep in bed alone. *Where were Valerie and Bethany?* She heard Bethany's voice murmuring when she hovered outside Bethany's room. She was on the phone, perhaps with the hospital or her husband.

Suddenly worried about her own nuclear family, Rebecca huddled in her bedroom and texted all her children. It was one in the afternoon, which didn't necessarily mean they would immediately text back. They were at work or at basketball camp or chatting with their friends at lunch.

Her simple text to all of them was the same. The sentiment was that she loved them. She missed them. And she wanted an update about what they'd been up to. Perhaps this wasn't fair since they didn't know she was back in Nantucket. None of them knew anything about Esme or Victor or Valerie or Bethany. Above all, none of them knew about Joel—the event that had splintered her heart until Freddy had found a way to put it back together again. *"You've been through so much,"* Fred had told her after they'd dated a few months. *"And I can tell you don't want to let me in. But listen, Rebecca. I'm here. I'm waiting for you. And I want to love you so badly, it hurts."*

Rebecca spent most of the day alone in her room. Occasionally, she heard one of her sisters or her mother walk down the hallway to the bathroom or go up and down the stairs, perhaps for snacks or drinks. The rain still hadn't let up, and Rebecca's heart was shadowed and grim. Once or twice, she allowed herself to look at photographs of her and Fred from last autumn when they'd taken a weekend trip to New York City to visit Lily.

Not for the first time, Rebecca considered her age. At forty-five, she wasn't old, but then again, she wasn't young. She felt caught in the middle of a story that had no ending. Had she been a widow in her seventies or eighties, she would have perhaps understood what to do better. Then again, her mother was sixty-nine and seemed no clearer on how to move forward than Rebecca did.

Around five, Rebecca walked downstairs and entered the dark kitchen. She sensed her sisters and mother in the house, portioned alone in their rooms. The morning had enveloped them in promise. *How could she bring them back together again?*

Rebecca set to work doing the only thing she really understood. She cooked onions, garlic, and peppers, rubbed spices into chicken, dropped oil into skillets, and hunted through the cabinets and refrigerator for ingredients. As she worked, she sang to herself, and the anxiety from the lonely day fell from her shoulders.

Suddenly, Rebecca heard a creak on the staircase. She froze, listening as someone came slowly from the second floor. She tried to pretend she hadn't heard anything and continued to stir and toss and salt. Moments later, Bethany peered through the doorway and smiled softly.

"Look at you," she said.

"I couldn't sit still anymore." Rebecca shrugged.

"What is it?"

"Butter chicken."

Bethany puffed out her cheeks. "You spoil us, Rebecca."

Rebecca listened as Bethany poured herself a glass of wine and walked to the window to peer out across the angry and darkening beach.

"What happened after I left?" Rebecca asked quietly.

"It was okay for a while. But soon, we got very quiet. I was thinking so much about Joel. About the beautiful memories I have before Dad left. And I started to cry. Valerie got upset and stormed into her bedroom, the way she did when she was younger. And Mom..." Bethany trailed off. "Well, Mom is devastated. She just lost her husband, and her moods are all over the place. After a little while, she fell asleep, so I left her alone. I've been on the phone with the hospital, checking on patients and med students who need me. My children both called. My husband..." Bethany paused for a moment, considering what to say. "Well, I wouldn't say my husband and I are on the best terms right now."

Rebecca's eyes widened. She hadn't expected this from Bethany, the "perfect Sutton daughter." But now, she remembered how little she knew about anyone in her family.

"Goodness, Bethany. I'm so sorry." She turned around and took in this view of her sister as she gazed out the window and drank wine.

"Maybe that's why I was so eager to get away," Bethany tried. "Our lives are so connected to my husband's family that it was easy to use that as leverage. It was finally time for me to reconnect with my family. And it was finally time for us to stop fighting every night of the week."

"Bethany..." Rebecca felt heartbroken.

But before she could think of the right things to say, more footfalls sounded on the stairs. Valerie appeared in the doorway, her eyes blotchy from crying.

"It smells delicious." Valerie sniffed. She poured herself a glass of wine and leaned against the counter, where she raised her glass to Rebecca and said, "It's so strange. I slip into my old patterns while I'm here. Like I suddenly become teenager Valerie rather than forty-one-year-old Valerie."

"I'm not sure if I believe 'growing up' is a real thing," Rebecca said.

"No. I've lived in many different cities and met all kinds of people. And the only thing that's sure is that nobody knows what they're doing or how to act," Valerie agreed. "I guess it's time I extend that same empathy to the Suttons."

"It's harder." Bethany nodded. "My own children think my husband and I should be perfect in all things. We're surgeons; we're involved in our community. We try really hard to live up to their expectations, but it's so much pressure some days. It means we take our fights to the garage, where they can't hear us."

Valerie frowned. "Do you think they'll figure out you're a real person with real problems soon?"

Bethany laughed. "Not if we can help it."

Suddenly, another set of footfalls was on the stairs. The three Sutton sisters froze, watching as Esme revealed herself in a pair of linen pants, a linen blouse, and a touch of lipstick. Looking regal and strong, she'd wanted to make an entrance.

"Mom," Bethany breathed. "You look gorgeous."

"And we look sloppy," Rebecca admitted, eyeing her leggings.

Esme waved her hand. "I don't have many memories of my mother. The ones I do have are of her always looking her best—no matter what the weather was, no matter if she was sad, no matter if she was sick. I think it was a trick of the mind."

"There must be something to that," Valerie agreed. After a pause, she added, "During my depressive episodes, I've hardly managed to dress myself in the morning. It definitely made everything feel worse. More hopeless."

Esme drew her eyebrows together and placed her hand on Valerie's shoulder. She searched for words that could take away the evident pain Valerie had gone through, but there was nothing.

Instead, she said, "I wish you would have been here. With me and Larry."

Valerie's eyes twinkled. "He was such a kind man."

"He really was the greatest man I ever knew," Esme agreed. She took another glass from the cabinet and poured herself some wine. "I'm glad you got to meet him."

The butter chicken was ready to eat. Rebecca procured four plates from the cabinet and set the breakfast table, as it felt cozier tucked in the back corner of the kitchen as the storm continued to boil outside. She filled their plates with butter chicken and refilled the wineglasses, then sat with her two sisters and mother and said, "I hope you'll enjoy." It wasn't lost on her that this was the first meal she'd ever made for her mother.

Rebecca watched Esme like a hawk. Slowly, Esme lifted a forkful of butter chicken to her lips, closed her eyes, and took a bite. She moaned and shook her head. "Rebecca. This is to die for!"

Rebecca couldn't help but smile. Esme squeezed her wrist. "You must give me the recipe," she added.

"It's not just the recipe," Bethany assured Esme. "Rebecca went to culinary school. She learned the secrets of the masters."

"Is it illegal for you to pass those secrets on to us?" Valerie asked.

"I swore I never would," Rebecca joked.

Slowly, they ate and talked quietly about everyday things. They talked about the weather, about Rebecca and Bethany's children, and about the approaching summer season and all the chaos it would bring to the island. Valerie spoke about her job as though it still existed, although Rebecca and Bethany were not sure about that. And Esme spoke about the Sutton Book Club as though it was not about to go under, although everyone at the table knew it would.

It was a conversation that hovered above reality for comfort's sake. And goodness, did they need it.

But after the plates were in the dishwasher and fresh glasses of wine were poured, Rebecca heard herself ask Esme, "Will you tell us about Larry?"

Emse's eyes were glassy. She gazed out the window for a long time and thought about what to say. "Larry and I met when I went back to college."

Rebecca was surprised. She hadn't known her mother had gone to college.

"As you know, I never finished my undergrad," Esme continued. "I was never fully focused, never really knew what I wanted to do, and then I got pregnant with Rebecca. Before I knew it, I had a baby, a husband, and this big house to care for. When I was in my late forties, I found myself alone here or alone at the Sutton Book Club with no one to talk to and nowhere to turn. Well, no one except your grandfather." She smiled to herself. "He urged me to take classes in anything I wanted to. So for two semesters, I lived in Boston and took classes at Harvard."

"Harvard!" All three of the Sutton sisters gasped.

"That's right," Esme said. "I took literature, writing, and French courses. Most of the students were in their twenties, of course, but a few here and there were like me —those who wanted to extend their education. Those who were a little bit lost. And one of those men was Larry Gardner. He was in my American literature of the twentieth century course. As though we were in our twenties, he asked me to help him write an essay. I went to his apartment, in which he'd lived since he'd gotten divorced. That night, he kissed me for the first time. I thought I would float away with happiness."

Rebecca was wordless. This was a story straight from a romance film.

"Mom!" Bethany gasped. "I had no idea."

Esme smiled. "I wasn't sure I deserved a second chance at love. What happened to your father and me was devastating. Truly. Although..." She trailed off. "Over the years, I began to make sense of why he left with Bree."

"No," Valerie said firmly. "What Dad did was wrong."

"Yes," Esme said. "It was wrong, and it hurt us very much. But he was broken."

"We were all broken," Valerie stammered.

"Which is why all of you took off for all corners of the

country and left me here," Esme said very quietly. "I can't blame you for doing that. You were young and angry, and you wanted to run away from your feelings. Your father did the same."

The table was very quiet. Nearly a full minute passed before Esme spoke again.

"I was so grateful to have another love, but I couldn't have imagined that Larry's and my love would last much longer than a semester," she said. "I was so pleased and blown away when Larry agreed to return to Nantucket with me and stay in the house where I'd raised my children. I couldn't bear to part with this place, as it felt like the last link I had with all of you. And after two semesters in Boston, I was ready to come home."

Rebecca remembered the rooms of that house that now felt like a museum. Her mother had needed those rooms to cling to whatever she had left of her children.

"Larry and I redecorated quite a bit of the house. I wanted to make him feel at home here," Esme continued. "And for many, many years, we were happy. Really happy. Of course, I still thought about you. I missed you. And I wished things could have been different." Esme trailed off and shook her head. "But Larry helped me deal with those feelings. He helped me go through time without as much pain."

Esme lifted her eyes to meet Rebecca's. Rebecca stirred with discomfort.

"Darling, I'm just so sorry to hear about your husband." Esme sounded breathless. "He left this world much too early. I imagine there's no way to get your head around it."

Rebecca blinked away tears and told herself not to make a scene. "I just worry so much about my children," she said, although they handled Fred's death far better than she did in many ways.

"Lily? Shelby? Chad?" Esme said Rebecca's children's names softly. Each syllable was heavy with purpose.

Rebecca's throat was very tight. "You would love them."

"I think I already do." Esme dropped her gaze. "I'd love the opportunity to meet them one day." She chuckled, then added, "As you can see, I haven't handled Larry's death very well at all. If you'll have me, I might need to lean on my daughters for support. At least for a little while." She was clearly ashamed to ask yet had no idea where else to turn.

"Mom, we're here. We're all here." Bethany reached across the table and took one of Esme's hands.

Esme shook her head. "I still can't believe it. These weeks have been a nightmare. In every way, I've been reminded of 1993 when your brother..." She paused, unable to continue.

Valerie's face crumpled.

"Dad came to see me," Rebecca said suddenly, surprising herself. "He was worried about you and wanted to make sure you were all right."

Esme furrowed her brow. This news was incomprehensible. It did not fit into the image she'd built of Victor Sutton since he'd left so many years ago.

"His marriage is over," Rebecca continued. "And I have a hunch he's a whole lot more lost than we can understand."

"Famous family psychologist Victor Sutton? Lost?" Valerie demanded.

Rebecca gave Valerie an icy look.

"Oh dear." Esme looked in disbelief. "When I made peace with his decision to leave, and when I met Larry and fell in love, I told myself over and over again that everything had happened for a reason." Esme grimaced, then added, "Well. That's a lie, isn't it? I will never believe Joel died for a reason. What good is a child's death? It's senseless. It's wrong. And it sent all five of us spinning in opposite directions for so many years, but when it comes to your father and me, I assumed we'd gone on to find our true-life partners. I suppose, then, it makes me sad that Bree and your father are divorcing. I wanted us to both have found meaning after all that heartache. I wanted everything to be okay."

For a moment, the table was silent. Rebecca found it difficult to breathe.

"Dad went to the hardware store today," Rebecca said suddenly, unsure of why she wanted to prove her father worthy of anyone's time. "He bought materials and tools for Doug and Ben and has promised to help them patch up that old house. It really is about ten seconds from being condemned. And Dad looked so peaceful as he began to hatch a plan of attack. I hadn't seen him like that since I was a little girl. It was strange that forty years of my life suddenly washed away, and I was five years old again, watching my dad work."

Esme's eyes were enormous. "Victor did what?" Slowly, she stood to her feet. "I have to speak with him. Is he in the guest room?"

Rebecca shook her head. "He went to his brother's tonight."

"Goodness. They don't get along in the slightest." Esme sat back down. Worry permeated her face. "He must really feel unwanted here."

Rebecca, Valerie, and Bethany were quiet. Decades of confusion and pain had eroded their once-powerful family. *How could they move on from this? How could they ever find peace?*

Chapter Twenty-One

Rebecca sat at the breakfast table the following morning with a mug of coffee and a croissant from the local bakery. Valerie hadn't been able to sleep, and after a very long walk, she'd returned with a big box of goodies, which she'd placed on the kitchen counter. Now, Valerie remained standing at the counter, typing furiously on her phone.

"So you had to leave that job in San Francisco?" Rebecca asked, sensing something amiss.

Valerie eyed Rebecca distrustfully. "I didn't love the way they handled their employees. Lack of trust. Lack of patience."

"That's terrible." Rebecca knew she wouldn't get to the bottom of what was really going on in Valerie's life because Valerie wasn't one for details. "Isn't San Francisco really expensive?"

"Crazy expensive," Valerie emphasized. "I don't know how people afford to live there." She put her phone down and rubbed little circles into her temples. "Mom loved the city when she first arrived, though. We walked endlessly in Golden Gate Park. I think she was trying to pretend she was better than she was. She hardly talked about Larry. In fact, she actually spoke about moving away from Nantucket, getting on dating websites, and trying to build a new life for herself. I now see how delusional she was."

Rebecca nodded. "I think we all have to tell ourselves stories to get through difficult times. That was the story Mom chose at the time."

Valerie nodded and sipped her coffee, clearly at a loss.

But before she could think of something to say, Esme breezed into the kitchen. She smelled of lilacs and soap. Her hair had been styled, and she wore cherry-colored lipstick. It was only eight in the morning, but she seemed ready to face the day.

"Good morning!" Esme poured herself a cup of coffee and eyed the croissants and other baked treats. "My goodness. Will every day with my daughters be a culinary surprise?"

"Valerie thought we deserved something nice," Rebecca said.

"Maybe we do, Val." Esme smiled.

"Where are you off to?" Valerie asked.

"Thank goodness I checked the calendar at the Sutton Book Club. I have a reading group coming at nine thirty to discuss *All The Light We Cannot See*. Twenty-five women! And they'll be expecting coffee and baked goods. The whole shebang."

"We'll help you," Valerie offered tentatively.

Esme's eyes shone. For a moment, Rebecca thought Esme would refuse their help. Instead, she said, "I can't imagine doing this alone. Thank you."

Within the hour, Rebecca, Valerie, Bethany, and

Esme were up at the Sutton Book Club. Coffee had been brewed, donuts, croissants, apple tarts, and cinnamon buns lined one of the long wooden tables, and they moved twenty-five chairs into a circle. June sunlight streamed through the large windows. The long shelves filled with books remained a stunning link to Grandpa Thomas, who, it seemed to Rebecca, blessed everything they did together as a family.

Amy Stevenson, a woman in her midsixties, was in charge of the reading group. She had poofy blond hair and an appreciation for sugary perfume. At nine twenty, she breezed through the front doors of the Sutton Book Club, took Esme by the elbows, and said, "Darling, I can't imagine how difficult it's been for you. I'm so glad to see you here. And I'm so glad you've managed to keep the Sutton Book Club open for us!"

Esme's smile was difficult to read. She spoke pleasantly with Amy, showing her the circle of chairs and the mass amounts of baked goods. All the while, Rebecca's stomach twisted with fear. Esme's sense of community and meaning were tied up in the Sutton Book Club. *How on earth could she raise over one hundred thousand dollars by the end of the summer? How could she avoid losing everything Grandpa Thomas had built?*

Rebecca pulled Valerie and Bethany into the kitchen. They stood in the shadows, listening as more and more women from the reading group mounted the stairs and greeted Esme and Amy.

"I think we should ask Mom about the bills," Rebecca said.

Bethany grimaced. "She's clearly upset. I don't want to push her into even more of an emotional downward spiral."

"But if we don't save the Sutton Book Club, what will she do? And how can we live with ourselves, letting our grandfather's legacy fall apart like that?" Rebecca demanded. It was suddenly the only thing in the world she cared about. She needed to make sure her mother still had the comfort of this remarkable place.

Valerie and Bethany exchanged glances. Before either of them could speak, however, Esme entered the kitchen and smiled. Under her breath, she gasped, "Goodness. Small talk takes a lot out of me these days." She then walked toward the sink and poured herself a glass of water. Her three daughters watched her like a hawk.

Finally, Rebecca heard herself speak. "Mom?"

Esme turned. "What is it, darling?"

Rebecca shifted her weight. "We know about the Book Club's money problems."

Esme's smile waned. She sipped the rest of her water, then clacked the glass on the countertop. Bethany's eyes were wide like saucers.

"I suppose you think it's something I need to make peace with," Esme breathed. "For everything, there is a season. A time to live. A time to die. And a time to close down the Sutton Book Club."

"No!" Rebecca cried.

Esme lifted her eyes, surprised.

"I mean, there has to be a way we can raise that money," Rebecca continued. "Valerie could probably throw the best party this island has ever seen. A fundraising event that could generate enough money to pay off your debts and keep the Sutton Book Club in business for many years to come."

Valerie gave Rebecca a panicked look. Esme turned to look at Valerie. "Could you really, Valerie?"

Valerie stuttered. "I don't know." But after another pause, she added, "I suppose I've planned fundraisers like that before. I don't know why I couldn't do it again."

"We'll brainstorm," Rebecca affirmed. "By the end of the week, we'll have a plan of attack. Maybe we can talk to the people you owe money to and get a small extension."

Esme furrowed her brow. "Larry repeatedly asked for an extension. I don't know how we thought we would ever make it work."

"But this time, we can show these people that we have a way to get the money," Rebecca explained even though she wasn't sure she believed in the plan herself.

Bethany nodded along with Rebecca, though her eyes were heavy with doubt. "It sounds great," she said.

Not long after the reading group began, Rebecca decided to leave the Sutton Book Club to go for a walk. The following evening was the meal she planned to cook for Ben and Doug, and she wanted to collect ideas for the kind of meal neither of them had experienced before. After she stepped out onto the front porch and took a breath of fresh air, Valerie stepped out onto the porch after her, her eyes fiery.

"Rebecca," she hissed. "How do you expect me to raise one hundred thousand dollars in just a couple of months?"

Bethany appeared in the doorway after that. She joined her sisters on the porch and shut the door behind her, grimacing.

"You don't think it's possible?" Rebecca asked.

Valerie grimaced. "I just don't want to get Mom's hopes up. Besides, I mean, even if I could generate that income over the summer, what about after that? The expenses on Nantucket have skyrocketed over the years."

Rebecca's stomach twisted. "Don't you think we owe it to Mom to try?"

Bethany and Valerie were wordless. Disheartened, Rebecca turned on her heel and hurried down the steps. Her thoughts burned with fears and ideas and uncertainties. For reasons she couldn't fully understand, she ached to see Ben again. She wanted to prove to him how worthy he was in her eyes through the food she cooked for him. Yes, the rest of the world had given up on him and Doug —but Rebecca thought she understood the depths of his loneliness and fears.

"Rebecca..." Bethany staggered behind her.

Rebecca turned to glare at her sisters. After a long pause, she said, "My life has gone off the rails. I have no husband and no restaurant, and my children are finding ways to grow up without me. I need to stay here. I need to help Mom. But neither of you are required to do that. Okay?"

Rebecca twisted back around and continued marching along downtown Nantucket's streets. She passed bouncing tourists, people who sat in the sun as they brunched, beautiful hotels in old-world colonials, and pretty girls in summer dresses. All the while, Bethany and Valerie followed her until she reached the harbor. There, she swung her arms over the warm railing and peered out at the sailboats as they shifted against the docks. Bethany and Valerie sidled up beside her. For a long time, no one spoke.

"Do you ever wonder what happened to Dad's boat?" Rebecca asked softly.

Valerie made a strange noise in her throat.

"The *Esme*?" Bethany asked. "I'm sure Bree didn't let him take that with him."

"What do you remember about Bree?" Rebecca asked.

Bethany groaned. "She was quite a bit younger than him, right? Late twenties or early thirties?"

"Can you imagine being that young now?" Valerie shook her head.

"She came over a few times for dinner," Rebecca said. "I assume that was before their affair started."

"I refuse to believe their affair started before Joel got sick," Bethany affirmed. "It's for my own mental health."

"Yeah. Me too." Rebecca watched as a young man carried his little girl along the docks. Her blond locks sparkled in the sun. "Bree seemed so magical to me back then. She was young and pretty, and she hadn't had children or gotten married, like every other woman I knew."

"Strange to think she must be around sixty by now," Valerie said.

Together, the three Sutton sisters walked the board-walk, each stewing in their own thoughts. Around noon, Esme wrote that the reading group had disbanded and that she planned to head back home for a nap before she had to be back at the Sutton Book Club for another meeting. Apparently, a group of teenagers met at the Sutton Book Club once per week to read Shakespeare to one another.

Eventually, Valerie demanded that they sit somewhere. Her feet ached. She pointed out a little wine bar along the water, and the three of them nabbed a table along the sands. A server came to take their order, and they asked for a bottle of sparkling rosé and three glasses.

In the distance, a boat cut along the horizon line, whizzing beneath a blue sky.

For a little while, the sisters were quiet. Rebecca made a grocery list for the Veterans' Dinner, which they'd planned for two days from now, as Bethany texted her husband and Valerie answered emails. Rebecca, too, texted with her children, who all reported they were having great summers but that they missed her. She was no longer necessary. She was no longer there to bug them about remembering their IDs or sports equipment or to get a good night's sleep.

But suddenly, Valerie hissed with surprise. Rebecca and Bethany looked at her, sensing something very wrong.

"You're not going to believe this," Valerie muttered.

"What?" Rebecca demanded as Valerie slid her phone onto the table with the screen up. Rebecca and Bethany leaned over to read the headline of the article.

RENOWNED FAMILY PSYCHOLOGIST NOT TO BE TRUSTED

Victor Sutton's face peered back at them. He wore a mysterious smile and what appeared to be the same suit he'd had on at Bar Harbor Brasserie.

In the article, the journalist discussed Victor Sutton's illustrious career, his rise to fame, his work with presidents and actors and talk show hosts. He spoke about Victor's incredible book sales and the world's constant belief in his message. "Victor Sutton was synonymous with truth, with wholesome family values, and with bettering ourselves. But now, Sutton's newly revealed dark past begs the question—should any of us have taken advice from him in the first place? How much damage has Victor Sutton done?"

"Oh no," Bethany breathed.

The journalist knew everything. He spoke of Victor's early days on Nantucket, of his first wife, Esme, and of his four children, Rebecca, Bethany, Valerie, and Joel. He wrote of Joel's death and of Victor's subsequent affair with Bree, with whom he ran away. "None of Victor Sutton's children have anything to do with him. As he's the number-one trusted family psychologist, shouldn't Sutton have found a way to patch up these wounds long ago?" The journalist even spoke of Valerie's failings in her industry as a way to "pin the blame" on Victor, which was enough to make Valerie's head explode. Bar Harbor Brasserie was mentioned as a "failed restaurant," as Bethany's story spoke only of her husband's very minor legal problems.

"What does my husband have to do with this?" Bethany hissed.

In every respect, the article dragged Victor and his family through the mud. It boggled Rebecca's mind.

"He must have known the article was coming out," Rebecca said suddenly. "He knew his reputation was about to be smeared, so he took refuge where he could. With me. With us."

Bethany and Valerie set their jaws. Nobody knew quite what to feel. Their anger toward their father and what he'd done was not a public thing. They felt exposed.

Rebecca scrambled away from the table and called Victor. *Had he seen the article yet?* She paced the fence around the wine bar and listened as the call rang out across the island. Unfortunately, he didn't answer, not the first, second, or third time she called. Remembering he'd promised to help Ben and Doug, she dialed Ben's number. Ben picked up on the second ring.

"Hi there!" He sounded jovial. "How are you doing?"

Rebecca's heart skipped a beat. "Oh. Fine, Ben. Fine. I was curious if you'd seen my father today?"

"He just left a little while ago," Ben reported. "The work he did on the house today was exquisite. He showed me a few techniques that should make things easier on me in the future. You wouldn't think that a psychologist like him would have such skills. I guess it's best never to judge someone at face value."

Rebecca's eyes widened. *Had Ben seen the article?*

"He didn't say where he was headed, did he?" Rebecca asked.

"He didn't. He did say he couldn't come by tomorrow. Something to do with his divorce?"

"Oh." Rebecca's head swam with curiosity. "Okay."

"But he did say he'd be back in two days," Ben continued. "Is he not answering his phone?"

"He's not," Rebecca said. "I hate to admit that I'm kind of worried about him."

"I saw him just about two hours ago," Ben assured her. "He seemed right as rain."

Rebecca thanked Ben and got off the phone. But when she returned to the table, she noted the article had been posted an hour ago. There was no telling how Victor was handling it. *Where had he run off to?* Ben had said, "Something about his divorce." *But what could that mean?*

When she asked her sisters, they shook their heads, at a loss. Valerie reported that already, Twitter was aflame with questions about Victor's capabilities as a psychologist. The hashtag was #ShouldWeTrustVic.

"People are tweeting stories about themselves," Valerie explained as Rebecca sipped her wine, exasperated. "They're talking about times they tried to follow Dad's principles, but they failed them. They still got divorced or lost custody of their kids or..."

"Gosh. That seems petty to me," Bethany breathed. "You could follow Dad's principles to a T and get different results every time."

"Are you suggesting you've read over Dad's principles?" Valerie asked, her eyes flashing.

Bethany stuttered. "I just glanced over them." After another pause, she added quietly, "My marriage is not always in the best state."

"Well, Dad's getting divorced for the second time," Valerie countered. "We don't even know why. Maybe he cheated on Bree with someone else?"

"If he left Bree for someone else, he wouldn't be on Nantucket with us," Rebecca pointed out.

"If we're going to 'trust Dad again,'" Valerie said with air quotes, "then we need answers from him. I want to know why he's really here. I want to know what he really wants from Mom and from us. Otherwise, I see no reason to let him back into our lives. He could be hanging around here, nursing his wounds until he can leave us again. And I made a pact with myself a long time ago never to let anyone fool me twice."

Chapter Twenty Two

That night and the one after that, the Sutton sisters didn't hear from their father at all. Together, they watched listlessly as the world noted Victor's previous grievances. The talk show host he'd helped through her custody battle took to her platform to say she was "listening to what the public had to say about Victor and would make an informed decision regarding her relationship with him going forward." To Rebecca, it was ridiculous. Victor's pain and torment had dictated his life thirty years ago, but wasn't it possible he'd learned and grown? Wasn't it possible he had the capabilities to heal so many of his patients, without fully knowing how to heal himself?

On top of not hearing from her father, Rebecca hadn't heard much from Lily in several days. Lily's lack of text messages hadn't initially been a worry to Rebecca. She was young, living her life in a huge city. But when Rebecca called to check in, and Lily sounded tired and flippant, Rebecca's heartbeat raced. As softly and timidly as Rebecca could, she asked her eldest if she was all right.

To this, Lily became irritated and volatile. "I'm fine, Mom. I've just got a lot on my plate. This internship is a big deal. You know?" After that, she found a way to get off the phone.

The morning after the article came out, Rebecca showed her mother the waterlogged books from Ben and Doug's place. Esme was mesmerized with them, flipping through the saturated waterstained pages and looking at the illustrations. "It seems like my father had books like these, too. I wonder where they went?" She set to work on drying them out, propping them in front of a large fan she dragged out of the basement. She told Rebecca there was no salvaging them for money purposes. "At least Ben and Doug can enjoy them for what they are—important historical artifacts. I assume they're brilliant stories, as well. If only I could read German!"

Two mornings after the article came out, it was time to prepare for the impromptu Veterans' Dinner. When Rebecca had asked Esme if the newly planned dinner was okay, Esme had smiled and said that there was a poetry reading at the Sutton Book Club that afternoon, but they would clear out by six. She then asked Rebecca if she could help her cook.

Now, Esme and Rebecca strolled through the busy stalls at that morning's fish market. A Nantucket local, Esme knew every single person there by name. Once, she stopped at the man who sold salmon and said, "Randy, you know, I found that book you were looking for. Why don't you come by the Book Club and check it out?" To this, Randy's eyes became wide, matching the smile on his face. "I can't believe you found it. That's such a help, Esme. My kid has been asking me about it for months." Esme's chest puffed out proudly when they walked from the stall with numerous piles of pink salmon. The man had given them forty percent off.

"You are such a pillar of this community," Rebecca said to her mother. They had paused for coffee a bit away from the fish market madness.

Esme smiled to herself. "I'm sure you're the same up in Bar Harbor."

"Maybe. Maybe I was. Fred and I were such a good team. But these days, when people see me, a light goes out in their eyes. They're terrified that what happened to me could happen to them, too. Like the bad luck will wash onto them."

Esme grimaced. "People can be so cruel. I remember something like that after your father left. Nobody could believe that my perfect marriage became sour. But people only see what they want to see. I'm sure you, Bethany, and Valerie have a far different memory from that time than I do."

"What do you mean?"

"We put all our love into Joel," Esme said simply. "We thought it would help him through. When it didn't, we couldn't return that love to each other anymore. It was a tragedy. But it wasn't anything you could explain to your neighbors or friends. Everyone thought we could use our love to pull through. But they didn't understand that, at that point, our love was a finite resource. And we both had had to find it in someone else."

Rebecca and Esme drove toward the Sutton Book Club with the fresh fish and ice packed in the coolers in the back. Early morning light streamed across the downtown streets and illuminated the shop windows. The mornings in coastal towns were beautiful and sleepy, as though no one was in a hurry to get started.

As they stored the fish in the Sutton Book Club in preparation for the night's dinner, Esme asked Rebecca, "Do you think you'll ever want to date again?"

Ben's face flashed through her mind for reasons Rebecca couldn't understand.

"I think I should get Chad and Shelby through school first," Rebecca answered instead. "After that, I can re-evaluate."

"You know, Nantucket High School isn't such a bad place," Esme said simply.

Rebecca's eyes widened. She hadn't thought for a second about moving to her island home. "I'm sure Shelby and Chad don't want to leave their friends."

"Of course," Esme said. "It was just a thought." She paused, then added, "Sorry to repeat myself, but I'd just love to meet them."

Rebecca recognized the pain behind her mother's eyes. She cupped Esme's elbow and said, "I know they'd love to meet you, too. It's finally time."

Again, she remembered Lily's strange voice on the phone. A pang of fear came over her, but she soon shoved it away. If Lily really needed her, she would call her. *Wouldn't she?*

That evening, Rebecca, Bethany, Valerie, and Esme gathered in the Sutton Book Club back kitchen to cook a Veterans' Dinner. As they sliced vegetables and water-melon and prepped clam chowder, salmon, crab cakes, and corn, Bethany explained she probably had to return home soon.

"It's been such a dreamy time," she said, her knife flashing over an onion. "But my hospital needs me."

Esme lifted one of her eyebrows. "You know, the Nantucket Hospital is not such a terrible place to work."

Bethany gave Esme a curious look.

"She's been pestering me about doing events here for years," Valerie admitted, smiling at Esme.

"We have to put something together by the end of the summer," Rebecca urged Valerie, and Valerie nodded even though they all knew it was a losing game. Even if Rebecca concocted a gorgeous fundraising event for the Sutton Book Club, no amount of money was truly sustainable. The state no longer provided; the world didn't care about books anymore. It was probably better to close the Sutton Book Club slowly and with dignity.

Very soon after, Ben and Doug arrived. If Rebecca wasn't mistaken, Ben had dressed up slightly and even styled his wild hair. They strolled through the Sutton Book Club and took their usual seats at one of the long, wooden tables. Valerie set up a Bluetooth speaker to play hits from the fifties and sixties, which got Doug's foot tapping. "I love this one," he said, smiling mischievously.

"How's it going?" Ben asked Rebecca as she floated out of the hot kitchen.

"Not bad!" Rebecca placed her hands on her hips. "We have quite a feast back there."

"You're too good to us." Ben's eyes glinted. "And you have to come by to see the work Victor's done on the house."

Esme's smile waned. "Victor was always such a handyman. I think he could have been happy working as a carpenter, but his parents were very hard on him. The Suttons were quite rich on the island, and they needed their boys to go into something prominent."

"Well, Victor Sutton certainly has made a name for himself," Doug said.

"An infamous name," Valerie said under her breath.

"Oh!' Rebecca snapped her fingers, remembering. "Mom set to work on drying out the old German books."

"I dried them out in front of fans yesterday," Esme explained. "And then placed some large paperweights on them this morning. I want them to sit for a good week before touching them."

"What a process," Ben said. "We can't thank you enough."

Doug was misty-eyed. He kept his lips shut as though he didn't want to acknowledge how much it meant. Rebecca knew he was ashamed for having allowed the books to fall apart like that in the first place.

It had occurred to Rebecca to look up what each book was worth, but she'd decided against it. Since the books were unusable, it was better not to know.

The rest of the veterans arrived by seven. The remaining Suttons and the veterans in the area sat at the two long tables, piled their plates with food, drank soda, coffee, and tea, and exchanged stories and laughed. One veteran asked Esme, "Two dinners in a week? Why did we get so lucky?" And Esme answered, "My daughter wants to cook for as many people as she can. It's a blessing and a curse for my waistline."

When they finished the dinner, Rebecca carried a stack of plates into the kitchen. Ben followed her with an even larger stack when she turned back. His smile was playful and endearing.

"You know, you should really open a restaurant," Ben said. "Nantucket could use your talents, and I could use a job washing dishes." He winked to make sure she knew he was joking. Still, Esme had explained to Rebecca how difficult it was for Ben to hold down a job.

"I used to have my own restaurant," Rebecca said, surprising herself. "But we had to close down."

"That's a surprise," Ben said. "I mean, it must have been crowded every night!"

"It was." Rebecca couldn't control herself. "But my husband died in January, and since then, it's just felt too painful to be there. I tried one night in May, but I completely fell apart." Relief flooded her. It felt wonderful to tell her story to someone who hadn't known her before this.

Ben's face fell. Before she knew what had happened, she found her face against his chest and his arms around her. Nothing about it was romantic. There was just the warmth of his body and the firm beating of his heart. They were two broken people struggling to go forward.

Suddenly, from the main room came the sound of Esme's voice. The rest of the veterans quieted. Rebecca lifted her head from Ben's chest and listened intently.

"Thank you for coming tonight," Esme began. "I can't begin to describe how much the Veterans' Dinner has meant to me over the years. As you know, my father was a veteran of World War II, and the men and women who served and continue to serve this country were very near and dear to his heart. Nobody quite understands the sacrifices you've made. And it's been my privilege to know you over the last several decades."

Rebecca lifted her eyes to find Ben's. Again, the tremendous pain within them struck her. *What had he seen? What couldn't she ever understand about him?*

Rebecca and Ben stepped toward the door that separated the kitchen from the rest of the Sutton Book Club. From the doorway, they watched as Esme continued her speech.

"This Veterans' Dinner is very special for me," Esme continued, "because all three of my daughters are here. Rebecca's in from Bar Harbor, Bethany's in from Savannah, and Valerie's in from San Francisco. As many of you know, my family hasn't had it easy. I don't suppose we've been very kind to one another all the time, either. But these days, we're doing our best to move forward with empathy and love. And that's something I'm grateful for." Esme placed her hand over her heart and locked eyes with each of her daughters.

Rebecca nearly collapsed with sorrow.

"The next thing I'm going to say is something of a surprise," Esme said. "I'm afraid that the Sutton Book Club itself is under tremendous pressure. There is a possibility we won't survive past the end of the summer."

The veterans in the room looked panicked and shocked. They eyed one another, incredulous. An older man raised his hand and asked, "Hasn't the state been providing for you? Aren't you a public service?"

Esme shook her head. "The state funds are no longer approved for the Sutton Book Club. It's anyone's guess why they were taken. Personally, I feel that community centers like this are no longer regarded as important, not when things like sports exist. It's not that I'm against sports. It's just that I think reading is the closest thing we have to magic, and I can't understand why parents and our government don't push our children toward books and libraries." Her eyes glinted with tears. "I'm sorry. I've done what I can here at the Sutton Book Club. I hope we can have a wonderful summer together. And then, whatever will be, will be."

Esme dismissed herself, hurrying from the room. At that, the veterans erupted with questions and conversation. Ben turned to look at Rebecca, and his cheeks were slack. "I don't understand," he breathed.

"It's not fair," Rebecca said. "A place like this should remain open indefinitely."

"And there's nothing we can do?" Ben asked.

"My sisters and I have been brainstorming. Maybe we can pinch together enough pennies to keep it open another year, maybe two. But that work might be so exhausting that it won't even be worth it."

Ben nodded and palmed the back of his neck. He looked devastated. Rebecca didn't know what to say. She headed for the table and collected more plates, urging the veterans to save room for dessert. Nobody seemed interested, though. Nobody wanted to talk about anything but saving the Sutton Book Club.

One after another, the veterans left. They shook Esme's hand and told her they would do everything they could to keep the place open. Esme nodded and thanked them. They all knew the veterans could do very little. One of the purposes of the Veterans' Dinner was to support them—not the other way around.

Ben and Doug were the last to leave. Again, Rebecca allowed herself to hug Ben. She had the startling realization that she wouldn't see much of him after this. Very soon, she would return to Bar Harbor and welcome Chad home from basketball camp. She would have to pick up the pieces of her adult life and figure out what was next.

Chapter Twenty-Three

That night, a chill overtook the island. Raindrops flattened against the windowpanes, and gusts of wind surged against the old house. Bethany placed logs in the fireplace and built a cozy fire, which the four Sutton women gathered around. They burrowed under blankets and watched the flames lick at the stones of the fireplace.

"Oh, but it was such a nice night," Esme repeated for the fourth time as though she wanted to assure herself of it. "I think it's good we told the veterans about our money troubles. It would have been wrong to close without warning them."

"There's no reason you can't have smaller Veterans' Dinners here," Rebecca pointed out. "Those people love you, Mom. They want to be around you."

Esme nodded. "I just don't know what I'll do with all of my father's books. I suppose I could sell them. Some of them must be worth something." Her eyes flickered with the light from the fire. She clearly wasn't pleased with the idea of selling her father's things.

Suddenly, there was a knock on the door. Esme leaped forward, but Rebecca stood first. "I can get it," she said.

"I don't know who would be out in this weather," Esme said.

Bethany and Valerie watched Rebecca like a hawk. Slowly, she unlocked the door and opened it just a bit. There, on the front stoop, stood Victor Sutton. He carried a massive plastic box, and raindrops painted his glasses.

"Dad!" Rebecca was amazed to see him after so much radio silence. She stepped back to allow him into the foyer. Upon entering, he placed the heavy plastic box on the rug, and Rebecca closed the door quickly.

Esme, Valerie, and Bethany were on their feet. They looked like soldiers, ready to defend their home. Victor removed his raincoat and hung it on the coatrack. To Rebecca, he looked smaller than ever as though the public's sour opinion of him had belittled him physically.

For a long time, nobody spoke. Rebecca wanted to throw her arms around him but held herself back. *Who was this man? This stranger? Was he anything like the father they'd had before Joel's death?*

"Where have you been?" Esme asked. She sounded breathless.

"We heard it had something to do with your divorce," Valerie said.

Victor blinked toward the ground. "It's true that I went to Providence. But it wasn't necessarily about the divorce."

"We read the article," Bethany breathed.

Victor's shoulders slumped.

"Did you know it was going to come out?" Bethany asked.

"I had a hunch," Victor said. "Bree was quite angry with me. She might have said a few things about my past to the wrong people."

"What did you do to Bree?" Valerie demanded.

But Victor just shook his head, clearly exhausted. "We were married for a long time. We had many trials and many happy times. But over time, something happened, as it sometimes does. I found myself falling out of love with her. The fact that this coincided with night-mares about Joel is difficult to explain. I woke up so often, sleepwalking through my house in Providence. I finally realized I was looking for him." His eyes were heavy.

Esme took a small step forward. "Oh. Victor..."

But Victor was too overwhelmed to look at her. Instead, he dropped to his knees and removed the top of the plastic box. "I went to Providence to get something from storage. I hadn't thought of these books in years."

Delicately, Victor removed each book one at a time. He then spread them carefully across the living room rug. There were eleven of them, each thicker and more alluring than the next. Each of them was beautifully illus-trated, from Germany, and so well-preserved that they were probably worth a fortune.

As Rebecca watched her father arrange the books in front of his family, tears spilled from her eyes. This was Victor's final peace offering. This was the last thing he had to give.

"My gosh." Esme shook her head, at a loss. "When Rebecca showed me Doug's books, I remembered that my father gave you his set as a wedding present. They were too delicate and important for the Sutton Book Club, and he asked you to take them. To care for them. And you did."

Victor nodded gravely. "I hadn't thought of them in years, not till I saw Doug's waterlogged ones. It never occurred to me to sell them, of course."

The Sutton sisters were flabbergasted. Slowly, Valerie, Bethany, and Rebecca dropped to their knees to look at the gold engravings on the tops of the books. Rebecca opened one to look at an illustration of a German forest with a small cottage tucked between the trees.

"I looked up what the books are worth," Victor explained timidly. "And it's enough to keep the Sutton Book Club open for another few years, at least."

Esme gasped. After a dramatic pause, she rushed for Victor and threw her arms around his neck. She shook violently. It was the first hug they'd shared in decades.

"Oh, Victor," Esme whispered, over and over again, as though his name had taken on new meaning. "I don't know how I'll repay you."

"Don't you get it?" Victor asked softly. "I'll never be able to make up for what I did."

After that, their hug broke. Victor wiped tears from his cheeks, turned, and walked down the hallway to the guest room. A moment later came the sound of his door closing. The Sutton women were left with the enormous books, which were symbolic in every way.

* * *

That night after everyone had gone to bed, Rebecca tossed and turned. She felt haunted by the events of that week, unsure if any of it had happened at all or what could possibly happen next. She also hated that Lily had answered her text messages with single words, as though she couldn't muster the strength to write more.

Rebecca planted her feet on the floor beside her bed. She was parched and decided to refill her water bottle in the bathroom down the hall. The clock on her phone told her it was one thirty in the morning, and the storm had finally quieted outside.

Like a ghost, Rebecca crept down the hallway. Just before she reached the bathroom, she realized a slick of light was coming from beneath one of the bedroom doors. It was Joel's.

Rebecca's heart was in her throat. Slowly, she stepped toward the door. *Who was in there? Was it possible she was dreaming that she'd gone back in time to 1992, and Joel had decided to stay up late to read or play with his toys?*

Instead, when she got close enough, she heard the soft murmurs of her parents' voices. Both of them were in there.

Rebecca couldn't make out everything they said. And she knew it wasn't kind to eavesdrop. But she clung to every word she heard. They calmed her.

"That must have been terrible to read," Esme said. "Who do you think Bree talked to?"

"We had a number of friends in the upper leagues of psychology," Victor said. "I can't tell you how many times she told me I should be more like Steven or more like Jackson or more like this or more like that. So I think, when I asked her if she really thought our marriage was working out, she wanted to take matters into her own hands. She wanted to show me just how little I mattered. And boy, did she have the ammunition to do that."

"That sounds hard," Esme breathed. "I can't imagine turning on my husband like that."

"Maybe you should have turned on me," Victor pointed out. "What I did was—"

"Don't," Esme said firmly. "I don't want to talk about it. Not in Joel's room."

They were quiet for a moment. Rebecca remained very still.

"It sounds like Larry loved you a lot," Victor said.

"He did," Esme agreed. "We had a very special connection. Gosh, I can't believe he's gone."

"When I learned he'd died, I knew I had to come find you," Victor said. "All I could think about was you, Joel, and our daughters. After all my work in the field, I knew none of us had dealt with Joel's death correctly. Even in losing Bree, I started to spiral."

"You can see it in Rebecca, can't you?" Esme asked.

"Fred's death uprooted her, I think," Victor agreed. "I'm sure Joel has been heavy on her mind since then."

Rebecca closed her eyes. *Did her parents see her so clearly?*

"Those poor kids," Esme said.

Rebecca didn't want to hear any more. She couldn't. Slowly, she abandoned her mission in the bathroom and returned to her bedroom, where she tucked herself in and stared at the wall. She went in and out of sleep for hours, imagining what else her parents said to one another only a few rooms away. It was one part nightmarish, one part beautiful. She hadn't realized how much she'd ached for her parents to see one another as humans again.

When she awoke again at five thirty, a series of text messages from Lily appeared on her cell. Rebecca was immediately wide awake.

LILY: I'm sorry to bother you like this. I know this is the greatest opportunity of my life. I know my future matters.

LILY: But I can't. I'm so lonely. I feel like I might die here in this tiny room alone.

LILY: And I'm so scared. And I miss Dad so much. And I don't know what to do.

LILY: I can't sleep. I can't eat. I'm just so tired, Mom.

LILY: I'm so tired.

Rebecca immediately called Lily's cell. Her heart was in her throat. She was overwhelmed with a single mission. She had to bring her children to Nantucket and figure out a way through this pain. She couldn't allow them to stew in sorry for thirty years the way the Suttons had. They were the Vances, and they would miss Fred forever. But somehow, they had to find a way to move on.

Chapter Twenty Four

L ily couldn't make it to Nantucket for another week. During that time, Rebecca called Shelby and Chad and explained that the family would take a much-needed vacation in Nantucket. "After the year we've had, we have to be together." Both Chad and Shelby understood. In fact, they sounded relieved. Further, Rebecca prepared one of the guest rooms for Lily and Shelby to share and set up a bed in the upstairs study, which was generally unused. Chad could sleep there.

During that week of Rebecca's preparations, Bethany returned to Savannah to perform several surgeries, see her children, and make peace with her husband, who'd more or less insinuated she'd abandoned the family. "I don't want to get divorced," Bethany had told Rebecca quietly. Her eyes were stormy. She said she would return soon to meet Rebecca's children and help tie up loose ends. Rebecca wasn't sure she believed her. Before Bethany left, Rebecca hugged her hard and said, "Let's not lose track of each other this time. Okay?" Bethany promised they wouldn't.

Valerie remained in Nantucket for the time being but was in talks to return to San Francisco soon to pick up where she'd left off at work. Although she still didn't fully trust Victor, she was impressed with the fact that he'd donated the antique books and subsequently saved the Sutton Book Club. She'd noticed the softness with which Esme and Victor spoke to one another, and she'd told Rebecca privately she "didn't trust it." To this, Rebecca had asked, "Yes, but what's the harm? They've been through so much together and apart. Why shouldn't they take refuge in each other for now?"

Esme and Victor went to an antiquarian to discuss selling the books. When they returned home that evening, they were vibrant and happy as though they'd spent the entire day laughing and telling stories. They reported that the antiquarian was "very optimistic" about the sale of the books. Many books like theirs hadn't survived the war.

Rebecca was strangely sad to leave Nantucket to pick up Lily. As she watched the island dissipate over the horizon, she couldn't believe she'd allowed so many years to go by between trips home. *How could she have given up on such a big piece of herself?*

During the six-hour drive to New York, Rebecca listened to audiobooks and albums she'd liked before meeting Fred. She wanted to get back in touch with the person she'd been before motherhood—before marriage. Maybe whoever she'd been would help her set the stage for who she would be next.

When Rebecca reached Lily's apartment, the door flew open and out popped Lily. She hugged Rebecca as though she was a drowning victim. When she stepped back, Rebecca found herself staring at a fragile person with sunken-in eyes and cheeks. It took every bit of restraint Rebecca had not to burst into tears. Instead, she said, "Are you all packed? Ready to go?" Lily nodded, grabbed her suitcase, and rushed down the hallway. She didn't look back.

The ferry returned to Nantucket around six thirty that evening. Rebecca watched Lily's face as she took in the vision of the island, a place she'd never been before. When they got off the ferry, Rebecca parked the SUV in a parking lot near the harbor, and together, they roamed the boardwalk, watching the boats and the tourists. Lily said, "I can finally breathe here. The air in the city was so stifling." At this, Rebecca took deeper breaths, trying to appreciate what she had.

After a while, Rebecca and Lily sat on a bench overlooking the water, and Rebecca tried her best to explain what had brought her to Nantucket in the first place. How could she wrap up thirty years of memories into a half-hour conversation?

Lily listened intently, her brow furrowing. When Rebecca told Lily about Joel, her eyes were fiery. She couldn't believe Rebecca had never told her children about their uncle! Rebecca apologized. She explained she could hardly look at her own pain, let alone translate that pain to the ones she loved most. "I ran away from everything that happened, but the pain caught up with me when your father died. Coming back here was a way to make peace with my own stories."

"Has it helped?" Lily asked.

Rebecca considered this. "I think I might be more brokenhearted than ever. But maybe that's healthier than pretending everything is okay."

Lily explained that she'd gone to New York City to pretend that everything was all right with her, as well.

Although she'd been a student in the city for years, she'd been mesmerized and disgusted with the rat race mentality, even at the intern level. None of those people seemed bothered by any of life's unfairness. None of those people had ever dealt with loss. "I woke up one morning and knew I was headed toward burnout," Lily said. "All I could do was cry in the bathroom. Isn't that pathetic?"

Rebecca shook her head and held her daughter close. She couldn't even begin to tell her how understandable that was.

Suddenly, a familiar face appeared in the crowd. It was Ben, and he looked fresh-faced, tan, and spry. Unlike normal, he walked alone, without Doug, and he wore what looked like a sailing uniform of shorts and a polo T-shirt. Rebecca hadn't seen him since last week's Veterans' Dinner, and her heart jumped into her throat.

"Ben! Hey!" Rebecca waved.

Ben made a beeline for Rebecca and Lily. Lily peered at Ben curiously.

"Ben, I want you to meet my eldest daughter," Rebecca said, praying she didn't blush too violently. "This is Lily."

Ben's smile was electric. "It's my lucky day!" He shook Lily's hand. "When did you arrive?"

"Just now," Lily said.

"Wow. I still remember my first day in Nantucket. I could tell immediately it was something special," Ben said.

Lily nodded but remained quiet.

"Where are you off to?" Rebecca asked.

"I just started a new gig," Ben explained. "I take groups of tourists around the island on sailboats. It's been pretty special to spend so many hours on the water."

"That's incredible!" Rebecca cried.

"It was your father's doing," Ben said. "He's been off the island a long time, but he seems to know everyone. When he heard I knew how to sail, he set me up."

Lily eyed Rebecca. "I've heard so many mixed reviews about him over the years," she said of Victor.

"You're going to love him," Ben said proudly. He then whipped his fingers through his hair. "Hey, I just finished my shift. Do you want to take a quick sunset sail? They said I can take the company boats out whenever I like."

"It's up to Lily," Rebecca said.

"How could I refuse a sunset cruise?" Lily joked.

Rebecca and Lily followed Ben to the sailboat, where they sat comfortably and watched as he untied the ropes and raised the sails. Rebecca hadn't been sailing in many years, but when she saw an opportunity, she jumped in to help Ben, tying sailors' knots with practiced ease.

"You know the bowline?" Ben seemed impressed.

"My father made sure I knew every kind of knot there was," Rebecca explained.

Ben studied the sails. They'd just slipped out of the harbor and rushed with the winds, heading eastward. Being this far from dry land was an incredible freedom. Rebecca had forgotten how delicious the salty air felt on her face. When she glanced at Lily, Lily had her eyes closed and her chin lifted as though she was praying.

"How old were you when Victor left?" Ben asked softly.

"I was fifteen," Rebecca said.

Ben shook his head. "Have you found a way to forgive him?"

"I don't know," Rebecca said. "But I think I'm slowly

finding a new way to love him. This version of him certainly deserves a second chance."

Ben's smile widened. Overhead, a bird stretched its wings and became a momentary shield from the sun. Out on the boat, Ben's muscles gleamed and flashed as he worked.

"How do you know my grandparents?" Lily asked Ben suddenly.

"I've known your grandma for years," Ben explained. "My roommate was in World War II, and he fought with your grandma's father."

Lily's jaw dropped. "How old is your roommate?"

"He's going on ninety-nine," Ben explained. "He's threatening to die on me every other day, but I think he's too stubborn to go." For a moment, Ben's eyes shimmered. It was clear that Doug's death would not be easy for him.

But he wouldn't be alone. Not now, Rebecca thought.

"Your father told Doug and me about the books," Ben said. "I'm so happy to hear the Sutton Book Club will be saved. That place saved my life. Maybe that's too dramatic to say, but it's true."

"Mom was telling me about these Veterans' Dinners," Lily said. "They sound fascinating. So many people who fought in so many different wars gathered together..."

"And your mother's cooking is to die for," Ben replied. "But I'm sure you already know that."

"I do." Lily was contemplative. After a moment, she asked, "So there's an entire working kitchen in the Sutton Book Club?"

"Yes," Rebecca said. "It's not as good as ours back in Bar Harbor Brasserie, but it's not bad, either."

"Why don't you have more consistent dinners there? You could even open up as a restaurant on certain nights of the week. That way, the Sutton Book Club would generate more income, and you could cook more often again," Lily suggested.

Rebecca and Ben locked eyes. Visions of Nantucket residents streaming into the Sutton Book Club to talk about books and art and music over delicious dinners filled her mind.

"I'm not sure," Rebecca said hesitantly. "Your sister and brother still have some high school to get through."

Lily's face was stoic. "Maybe it could just be a summer experiment. We'll be here on the island, anyway. And Shelby, Chad, and I can help out however you need."

"I'll be available, as well," Ben affirmed.

"It's not like you won't be cooking up a storm, anyway," Lily teased. "Why not show off your skills to the people of Nantucket? Let them know what they've been missing since you went away."

Rebecca's heart lifted. She slung her arm over Lily's shoulders and shivered with excitement. "We'll have to talk to Shelby and Chad about it," she said.

"How could they say no?" Lily asked. "All we want is for our mother to be happy again. We want to hear you singing in the kitchen like you always did before."

Chapter Twenty Five

C had and Shelby arrived at the Boston airport three days later. After the short drive from Hyannis Port, Rebecca and Lily waited for them, waving wildly as they walked out of arrivals. They were both suntanned and toned and clearly overwhelmed, their backs heavy with backpacks and their eyes alight. As a family of four, they held each other in a big group hug as the rest of the airport guests milled around them. Although Chad tried to pretend he wasn't crying, there wasn't a dry eye in the group. It had been a terrible decision to break their family up over the summer. Rebecca was so glad they'd rectified that.

Back at the old Victorian home, Esme had baked enough cookies for thirty-five grandchildren rather than just three, and she hugged Chad and Shelby as though it was more of a reunion than a first meeting. She already loved them to bits. Victor soon retreated from the study to greet them. The divorced grandparents and grandchildren sat around the kitchen table together, ate cookies, drank milk, and talked about the first few weeks of their summer vacations. Nothing had gone as planned. Shelby said there had been an outbreak of bedbugs at the camp in the Acadia Mountains, and she'd spent more time cleaning bed sheets than hiking. Chad had twisted his ankle during day three of basketball camp but hadn't wanted to worry Rebecca, so he kept the news to himself. Rebecca hated this. She wanted her children to feel they could tell her anything.

Still, she understood wanting to protect your parents. Esme and Victor were damaged people, and she wanted to help them in any way she could.

Since Lily had arrived in Nantucket, Esme had become a full-time grandmother. She'd spent hours with her at the kitchen table as they'd spoken about Lily's time in New York City, her hopes for her future, and how much she missed her father. Rebecca sometimes partici-pated in these conversations; other times, she was upstairs, fine-tuning the menu she wanted to feature for the first night of The Sutton Book Restaurant.

Esme, Victor, and Rebecca had decided upon a soft opening for the restaurant the night of June twenty-third, which was only a few days away. Already, Lily, Rebecca, and Ben had walked all over town, hanging signs to adver-tise the event. Because the Sutton Book Club only had two very long tables, they'd purchased ten smaller tables to place around the old colonial home, along with fake candles to give more ambience to the atmosphere. When Lily had suggested they use real candles, Rebecca and Esme had cried at once, "No! The books!" Lily had made fun of them ever since, repeating that phrase with more and more emotion. "No! Not the books! Save the books!" she'd cried, like a soap opera victim.

Unfortunately, Bethany was back in Savannah, and

Valerie had returned to San Francisco. After Chad and Shelby arrived, Rebecca introduced her children over video chat. They sat and ate cookies in the kitchen with their grandmother and waved at Valerie and Bethany with confusion marring their faces. Who were these aunts they'd never known? Both Bethany and Valerie promised they'd come out to Nantucket soon to meet them. Rebecca's heart ached for her sisters, just as it always had since she'd left Nantucket. How she loved them! How she wanted to know them her entire life.

The day before the soft opening of The Sutton Book Restaurant, Victor was in the kitchen bright and early. There was confidence in his smile, and he spoke to everyone in the house with ease. Esme sat at the kitchen table with a newspaper in front of her, and she smiled as Rebecca entered.

"Victor? I need seven for a French castle." Esme tapped her pen to the right of the crossword and eyed her ex-husband.

"Château," Victor said without a moment of thought.

Esme smiled in a way that hinted she'd known the answer already; she'd just wanted Victor to be involved. "Thank you," she said as she wrote the letters in the little boxes. "How did you sleep, Rebecca?"

"My daughters were giggling in the room next door," Rebecca said as she poured herself a mug of coffee. "I think they're happy to be back together again."

"I'll say. Isn't it marvelous that they're such good friends, despite being four years apart?" Esme said. "Shelby looks at Lily the way Bethany and Valerie used to look at you, you know. Like you were a goddess or a queen."

Rebecca felt a pang of sorrow for her childhood. She

sat across from her mother as Victor poured himself a bowl of cereal and a touch of milk. She was so lost in thought that she hardly heard him when he spoke.

"I'm sorry? What was that?" Rebecca asked.

"I was hoping you and the kids would come with me this afternoon," Victor explained again. "I have a surprise."

Rebecca cocked her head. "Do you know about this?" she asked her mother.

Esme shook her head. "I don't know anything. But I'm unfortunately busy today with Book Club obligations."

"I've told her I'll surprise her separately," Victor explained. "As long as you and the kids keep it a secret." There was a childlike and mischievous look in his eyes. Rebecca had absolutely no idea what he had up his sleeve.

* * *

That afternoon, Rebecca, Lily, Shelby, and Chad piled into Victor's car, which he'd brought back from Providence. The kids were stuffed in the back seat, just as they'd been in the golden days when Rebecca had to take them to basketball, ballet, piano lessons, and art classes. Eventually, she'd wised up and gotten the SUV.

It was a beautiful day on Nantucket. The storms of the previous few weeks were now nothing but a memory. Victor drove them through downtown streets, laughing at the tourists as they crossed at-will, regardless if vehicles were there or not. "I think when people go on vacations, they lose their minds," he said.

"Is this a vacation for us?" Chad asked from the back seat. "Or is this more of a lifestyle change?"

As Victor turned the car onto the road nearest the harbor, Shelby and Chad peered out the window at the enormous field of tilting sailboats.

"I hope it's a lifestyle change," Shelby joked, then quickly adjusted. "Not that I don't love Bar Harbor. I do!"

"We all love Bar Harbor," Lily affirmed. "But you have to admit something's special about Nantucket."

"That there is," Victor said wistfully. "And your grandmother's and my families have been on Nantucket for generations. Your blood is here."

Victor parked the sailboat two minutes from the harbor docks and burst from the driver's seat. Rebecca and her children got out of the car and followed his confident strides toward the docks. Rebecca's heart had begun to beat very slowly; memories hovered around her, heavy and light at the same time. She could almost trick her mind into thinking Joel was just up ahead of them, skipping along the dock as the sunlight danced on the water.

All at once, it was before them—a glorious sailboat with the name *ESME* painted on the side. Rebecca's throat was very tight. Nostalgia was a powerful thing. She touched her father's arm and whispered, "You've had it all this time?"

Victor nodded, unable to look at her. "I put it in storage all those years ago. She needed a bit of TLC, but she's in working order now. She'll be out on this dock all summer long if you want to sail her." Finally, he turned to find her eyes. "I know you're a good sailor. You always amazed me."

Lily, Shelby, and Chad were impressed with the boat. Fred had never owned one, as the water around Bar

Harbor was always more tumultuous. He had preferred the mountains to the seas.

"Shall we take her for a spin?" Victor asked his grandchildren.

They cried out with excitement and boarded. Lily's and Shelby's hair flashed around with the wind off the sound. Victor mounted afterward and headed for one of the ropes. He then pointed for Rebecca to untie the opposite one, just as he'd done when she'd been a girl.

When the boat was safely out on the water, rushing through the waves as the Nantucket sun burned above them, Victor surprised them with a picnic. He looked jolly and eager as he passed around sandwiches, fresh fruit, nuts, and chips. Rebecca had never once imagined what her father might have been like as a grandfather. It turned out, he was pretty good at it.

When Victor was preoccupied with something on his phone, Rebecca gazed at her children, who nibbled on their sandwiches and watched the water. It had always amazed her how painful it was to love the ones you loved most. It was a physical ache.

"Do you want to learn how to tie a few sailor knots?" Rebecca asked suddenly.

Her three children nodded eagerly and watched as she lifted a spare rope and began to twist it into the bowline and the reef knot and the clove hitch. They were mesmerized and soon came over to try their hand at each knot. Rebecca felt proud to show them this element of her past. Several paces behind her, she could feel her father watching her, terribly proud to be there.

So much had happened. So many eras had passed them by. But a sailor's knot was still a sailor's knot. They were still tied the same way as ever before.

* * *

That night on the back porch, Chad slathered his face with lotion and laughed that he'd let his cheeks burn. Rebecca poured her children glasses of water and supplied snacks. Together, the four of them sat and watched as orange and pink light played over the horizon and turned them over to darkness.

For not the first time that week, Rebecca forced herself to tell the story of Joel Sutton. She explained to her two youngest how difficult Joel's death had been on the Sutton family and how they'd never really dealt with it. She watched Shelby and Chad for some sign of breakage or distrust. But instead, they just showed how truly sad they were—not to have known Joel and not to have understood the depths of their mother's pain.

Soon, Lily, Shelby, and Chad began to recite their favorite stories of their father. They told his favorite stories, talked about his favorite foods, and remembered him for the delightful, hilarious, complicated, and marvelous person he'd been. Rebecca spent the evening alternating between laughter and tears.

"I don't want us to pretend this terrible thing never happened," she said slowly. "My parents and sisters and I never spoke about Joel, and that turned Joel's death into a mountain of unspeakable pain. We have to be open about how we feel. We have to acknowledge what he meant to us."

Her children nodded. Lily reached across the table and took her mother's hand. "We'll always be together," she told her softly.

Rebecca nearly broke down after that. Her biggest fear had been that her own children would run away from this pain, just as she had from Joel. She didn't deserve how good they were, but God, she was grateful for it.

* * *

The following early afternoon, Rebecca and Esme began to set up for The Sutton Book Restaurant. They placed tables with white tablecloths and decorated them with beautiful china. Already that evening, sixty people had reserved seats around The Sutton Book Restaurant, and they would host up to twenty-five at a time. It was exhilarating. Esme also hoped everyone would rent out a book when they left. "Maybe we could even recommend a book to pair with their meal?" she suggested. Rebecca loved the idea, and Esme set to work. It was her lifelong duty to get people excited about reading again.

Rebecca was nervous. Yes, she'd had a restaurant of her own before. But back then, Fred had been her backbone, her strength. Now, she had to rely on her family, who had very little restaurant knowledge. Her children, the servers for the night, assured her they would do as she said, whenever she said it. Then they laughed and called her "chef," just as they always had. This lightened her mood a great deal.

The menu for the evening was fit for any night at Bar Harbor Brasserie. The starter was a French mussels pot followed by a clam sauté, a blue lobster Catalan, and a Hokkaido scallop grain. She planned to finish the dinner with her favorite dessert, a crème brûlée. *Who could resist?*

When Rebecca explained the menu to Esme, Esme's eyes got progressively larger and panicked.

"I haven't even heard of half of those words, Rebecca," Esme said.

Rebecca laughed and fanned herself with her hand. "Don't make me more nervous than I already am!"

Midway through prep, Ben arrived. Rebecca had invited him to help slice and dice vegetables and fish, and then she'd promptly cursed herself for asking him. *Who was she kidding? She couldn't have a silly crush.* But Rebecca's heart nearly shattered when he breezed through the kitchen door and flashed her that handsome smile. She handed him a knife, and he set to work with his head down. He explained that he genuinely liked to work hard, but that his PTSD had gotten in the way of so many of his career options.

"How is the sailing job going?" Rebecca asked.

"It's the best job I've ever had," Ben explained. "It helps to be outside. To feel the sun on my face and breathe the salty air. When I get home, I feel rejuvenated and ready to talk to Doug, to tell him jokes and go for a walk and cook dinner. Having a house without so many holes in it has also been great for our moods. Victor really came through."

Rebecca slid onions into a skillet. Her smile made her face ache. Many, many years ago, when she'd fallen in love with Fred, she'd been a young woman reeling from the broken hearts of her youth. Now, she was a middle-aged woman, and she was still reeling.

A few hours later, Esme called into the kitchen to report that the first guests had arrived. "Lily's already out there asking for their wine order!"

Rebecca and Ben locked eyes. Rebecca felt exhilarated and anxious all at once. Perhaps if she'd been a different sort of person, less afraid, she would have kissed

Ben on the cheek and wished him luck. But as it stood, she wasn't ready.

What she really needed was a friend.

As Rebecca prepared the first course for the first couple, the skillet screamed and hissed. Ben continued to prep, his eyes alight with excitement. There really was nothing like being in the kitchen of a restaurant. The adrenaline was wild.

"Ben?" Rebecca couldn't take it anymore. She had to say something.

Ben turned to catch her eye. She could feel it; something was happening between them.

"I just wanted to thank you for your friendship," Rebecca said. "It's been the hardest and loneliest year of my life. But I couldn't have imagined the past few weeks without you."

"It's been quite a time," Ben agreed. "I suppose it goes without saying how lonely I've been over the years. But right now..." He paused and looked at his chopped onions. "Right now, I don't feel so lonely. I feel alive. And as a veteran, you don't know how rare that feeling is."

Rebecca was captivated by him. She was fascinated by the stories he'd already told her and the ones still to come.

But already, Chad and Shelby were in the kitchen, telling her what their new guests had ordered. Wine needed to be poured, and the beer needed to be procured from the fridge. Esme hustled about, performing these duties. Lily, Shelby, and Chad spoke with authority; they knew that how they operated the first night of The Sutton Book Restaurant would dictate how the island of Nantucket regarded the restaurant as a whole. The restaurant had to work as it would ensure revenue for the Sutton Book Club.

The kitchen was alive. Every burner was red with heat. Steam fogged up the windows. Rebecca's children whisked in and out, carrying beautifully-plated courses. And all the while, Ben worked diligently beside her, following her lead. Esme, too, was a trooper, pouring wine like a maniac and making jokes as she went.

Only once, midway through the third and fourth courses, did Rebecca, Ben, Esme, and all of the Vance children find themselves in the kitchen at the same time. The franticness of the evening made them quick to laugh. Outside, a burning sunset was brilliant with nostalgia. Shelby giggled at something Chad said and punched him in the upper arm, as Esme reported that everything was going "great. Just great. I can't believe we haven't done something like this before."

Suddenly, Rebecca felt a song coming from her heart and soul. The lyrics for "Sentimental Journey," first sung by Doris Day, swelled from her lips.

"Mom always sings in the kitchen," Lily said with a smile. "It's her thing."

"And this is one of her favorites," Chad reported.

Esme and Ben stopped short and watched her before they, too, began to sing. Even her children knew the lyrics, and they joined in before they had to race back out to their tables and tend to the guests.

As Rebecca continued to sing and prepare the plates for the guests, Esme placed her hand on Rebecca's shoulder. Her eyes welled with tears. "Your grandfather sang that song all the time," she whispered.

"I remember," Rebecca said. "I guess it's where I got it from."

"Doug sings it sometimes, too." Ben was close to breaking down. "It was the song they listened to at the end of World War II. The song reminded them they would soon be home with their loved ones. That so many people at home loved them and rooted them on."

"And here we are together," Esme breathed. "We're home. We're safe. And we have all of them to thank."

The Sutton Book Club was full of diners who ate and laughed. Fake candlelight danced on their cheeks and in their eyes. They shared stories and shared plates and told each other they couldn't possibly eat another bite, yet they still managed to eat several more. When Rebecca looked back later, this was one of the greatest nights of her life, as it was the night when she remembered who she was, who she'd always been, and who she could possibly be. She was Rebecca Sutton Vance. She'd loved, and she'd lost. But she remained standing in the heat of her kitchen, cooking her art. As long as she had this, she would remain true to herself forever.

Coming Next in The Sutton Book Club

Pre Order Trick of Light

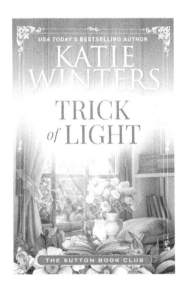

Other Books by Katie Winters

The Vineyard Sunset Series

Secrets of Mackinac Island Series

Sisters of Edgartown Series

A Katama Bay Series

A Mount Desert Island Series

A Nantucket Sunset Series

The Coleman Series

A Frosty Season Series

Connect with Katie Winters

Amazon
BookBub
Facebook
Newsletter

To receive exclusive updates from Katie Winters please
sign up to be on her Newsletter!
CLICK HERE TO SUBSCRIBE